I0574012

MERRY SCROOG-MAS!

A HOLIDAY ROMANCE COLLECTION

KARI LEE HARMON

OLIVERHEBERBOOKS

All rights reserved.

No part of this publication may be sold, copied, distributed, reproduced or transmitted in any form or by any means, mechanical or digital, including photocopying and recording or by any information storage and retrieval system without the prior written permission of both the publisher, Oliver Heber Books and the author, Kari Lee Townsend, except in the case of brief quotations embodied in critical articles and reviews.

PUBLISHER'S NOTE: This is a work of fiction. Names, characters, places, and incidents either are the product of the author's imagination or are used fictitiously. Any resemblance to actual persons, living or dead, business establishments, events, or locales is entirely coincidental.

Copyright © Kari Lee Townsend

Published by Oliver-Heber Books

0 9 8 7 6 5 4 3 2 1

NAUGHTY OR NICE

CHAPTER 1

"Drinking these things is not a good idea," Samantha Darling said, swirling a candy cane through her Peppermint Martini.

"Live a little. It's the holidays," her elfish friend, Ellen Patterson, responded. "It's been a year, babe." She tossed back her fiery red hair and swallowed half her drink in one gulp, then winked her forest green eyes. "Forget Mark's sorry ass and move on."

"His ass *is* sorry, and I have moved on." Samantha took a tentative sip. The minty flavor sliding over her taste buds was surprisingly good, but her eyes watered just the same.

"Ellen is right, Sam," her other friend, Amber Evans, chimed in. Amber was the total opposite of Ellen—Amazon tall, dark brown hair, and whiskey-colored eyes. "You're always so *nice*, but that only got you cheated on and dumped."

"Gee, thanks." Samantha frowned.

"You've thrown yourself into your work and forgotten how to have fun," Ellen said.

"It's time you got back in the game," Amber added.

"I'm happy being single." Samantha took another sip, wincing less this time.

Ellen pointed her finger at Samantha. "We love you, but you need closure, babe."

"Puh-lease." Samantha brushed Ellen's finger aside. "I'm fine. It's just today."

"Right," they chimed like a mismatched set of bobsy twins with bells.

Samantha smirked. "What's this, an intervention?"

"Of sorts." Amber patted her hand.

"Mark *ruined* my Christmas last year. You guys know how much I love Christmas." Samantha met their eyes. "I really thought I'd be celebrating my first wedding anniversary, but here I am with only memories of him and that woman in our bed with festive Christmas condoms, for Christ's sake. I carry the stupid things in my purse to remind me of what an idiot I almost married." She tipped up her drink and drained the contents without a single wince this time. The straight liquor warmed her throat on its way down to join its many friends in her belly.

"Just because you two looked good together doesn't mean you *were* good together," Ellen said. "I never liked the guy. Why not get the cheating bastard back by using those festive condoms with"—she searched the room until her gaze landed at the end of the bar—"Mr. Tall, Dark and Sexy who just sat down."

Ellen waggled her fingers at the gorgeous dark-haired man who filled out every inch of his expensive suit. He wore a serious expression on his tan chiseled features as he talked to two other men. His dark gaze snapped to Ellen's hand, and Amber held up her glass and pointed to Samantha.

"Stop that." Samantha grabbed their arms then met the man's piercing stare, feeling the impact in places she hadn't felt anything for a very long time.

Her breath hitched. He really was gorgeous, but big and intimidating. She felt her blush flame over her face as she gave him a little shrug. He arched a thick black brow and then turned his back on them all.

"Ouch," Amber said.

"Oh my God, that was so embarrassing." Samantha fanned her neck and slid her empty glass away.

"Screw Tall, Dark and Stuffy," Ellen scoffed.

"Or not." Amber wrinkled her nose. "His loss."

Christmas shoppers and people getting off work had filled every inch of the popular Boston bar known for its Friday happy hour. Stuffy had looked oddly familiar to Sam, but forget him. He'd shot her down. Not that she was actually interested, but he didn't have to make it so blatantly obvious he *wasn't*.

Having met after work from the same advertising firm and still dressed in their suits, the women weren't ready to go home yet. They kept their butts planted to their stools, even though they'd been there for hours and had consumed more Peppermint Martinis than any sane person should.

"I've about had it with men. Getting the cheating bastard back is starting to sound yum-may in my tum-may." Samantha giggled, clinking glasses with Ellen. Whoa, boy, those mint 'tinis were kicking into overdrive now.

"I'll bet we can find someone to jingle your bells." Amber looked around the bar. "Help you forget all about that ex-of-yours."

"No, no, no." Samantha waved her hand in front of her face

and nearly fell off her stool, which drew another intense stare from Mr. Stuffy. She mimicked his actions by arching her brow high and turning her back on *him*.

"Mark doesn't live in Boston anymore, so it's not like he'd even find out." Samantha slurred her words. "Besides, I'm just not ready."

"There are other ways to get closure, though I can't think of a more pleasurable one," Ellen pointed out.

"I can't believe I'm agreeing with her again," Amber glanced at Ellen, "no offense, hon, but you do have some outlandish ideas."

"None taken," Ellen stated, point blank. "Sam could use a little outlandish right now."

"Landish, landish, bobandish. Banana, fana, fofandish. Me, my, momandish," Samantha giggled, sweeping her hands wide as she sang the grand finale off-key, "Laaaaaan-dish." Oh Lordy, those drinks had moved way past 'kicking in' to flat out taking over.

"Oh-kay." Amber quirked a brow. "Just be a little naughty. A little less goody-two-shoes."

"Goody, goody, boboodie—" Samantha started, but Ellen slapped a hand over her mouth. Who knew Ellen was such a strong little elf?

"Didn't Mark run off with the hussy on the outskirts of town somewhere?" Ellen asked.

"I don't remember the town, but I remember the hussy's shop," Amber answered. "Stowe's Boutiques. It isn't that far from here as I recall."

Samantha peeled Ellen's hand from her mouth. "Yeah, so, bobo?" She grinned at both of them.

Ellen frowned. "So, *bobo*, go do something. Embarrass him

like he did you. That way all the people he's duped in that small town will find out what he's really like. What could Santa possibly do to you that Mark hasn't already done?"

"Spank me like the bad, bad girl that I am. Whoops, did I say that out loud?" Samantha stifled a snort, slapping her own hand over her mouth. Damn abstinence did crazy things to her mind when under the influence, apparently.

"Good Lord, I think we overdid it, Ellen."

"Overdid what?" Samantha slurred, eying them suspiciously.

"Nothing. Just, whatever you do, don't do it tonight. You really are a lightweight." Amber flagged down the bartender and paid off their tab.

"For once, I agree with her." Ellen shook her head. "You ain't got the balls to deck the halls, babe."

"Awww. I really wanted to deck Mark's balls," Samantha said, then scrunched up her face. "That didn't come out right, did it?"

"Uh, not so much, but if we see Mark, we'll gladly give him the message." Amber helped her to her feet while Ellen called a cab. "Come on, hon, it's time to go."

As they led her to the door, Mr. Tall, Dark and Stuffy followed, his eyes meeting Samantha's with an amused albeit curious stare. She looked him up and down, then stuck her nose in the air and waltzed out the door with her head held high. She could have sworn she heard him chuckle behind her.

His loss, indeed.

Moments later, after insisting she was fine on her own, Samantha sat safely tucked in the back of a taxi with the driver asking, "Where to, ma'am?"

The last place she wanted to go was home alone. She didn't

want to be safe anymore. The girls were right. It was long past time she quit hiding and began living again.

"Meter's running, lady. Where to?" the cabby repeated.

She narrowed her eyes, and her lips tipped up at the corners. Maybe she did need closure, and she had the perfect idea for what to do with those festive condoms. Leaning back, she settled in, then slurred off, "Stowe's Boutiques." She might not have the balls, but knew a thing or two about decorating a hall.

She was an advertising exec, after all.

UGH! Being naughty was overrated, Samantha thought as she struggled to open her eyes, the blinding light making her headache worse. Peppermintinis might taste yummy going down, but they left a skunky taste in your mouth the next morning and sure packed a hell of a hangover punch.

She held on tighter to the man her arms were wound around, his facial hair tickling her cheek as she tried to go back to sleep. Wait a minute. Tall, Dark and Stuffy didn't have a beard. She had a sinking sensation this wasn't her bed, and she was no longer dreaming. Running her hands over what felt like genuine velvet, she thought, *Oh, boy.* This wasn't a man, either. He was too hard and not in a good way.

Samantha lifted her pounding head to look straight into Santa's eyes. She had crawled into his padded wooden lap, and now her stiff joints and sore butt were paying the price. Only she wasn't wearing her clothes. She glanced down at her outfit and chewed her bottom lip. Oh, no. She was wearing Mrs. Claus's outfit. Then that meant...

Afraid to look but having no choice, Samantha glanced to the side and winced. Yup, just as she'd feared. She'd dressed Mrs. C in her underwear: black lace bra, matching thong, and garters, as Mrs. C fixed her blank stare on Samantha while holding her martini glass in her hand like a well-earned trophy. Samantha's thong looked like string as it cut deeply into Mrs. C's padding.

"Sorry, Mrs. C," Samantha whispered, holding her head so it wouldn't fall off. She glanced at the elves, who were hard at work, and repeated, "Lord, am I sooo sorry." Samantha gulped, staring at her handiwork in horror. She'd undressed each one, making them look like a page right out of a twisted fairy tale: "Mrs. C and the seven castrated freaks."

Elfish manikins were not anatomically correct.

Samantha had positioned them in precarious poses, resembling The Village People gone wild. Their jolly little faces grinned wide as they massaged parts of Mrs. C no elf should *ever* be allowed to touch.

Samantha groaned, wanting to crawl into a corner and die. She remembered sitting on Santa's lap, pretending he was Mark, and lecturing him about what a no-good hussy Mrs. C was. Damn peppermint poison, she thought when another thing struck her. If Mrs. C was wearing Samantha's underwear, then that meant Samantha must be buck naked beneath all that fur, apparently giving jolly 'ole St. Nick a lap dance he wouldn't soon forget.

"Merry Christmas, Big Guy," she muttered and could have sworn his eyes twinkled. Her cheeks heated and turned as rosy as his. She must have passed out before she had a chance to make her getaway.

Mark would probably be here any moment, and she did

not want to be caught in this predicament when it happened. Samantha struggled not to throw up and held her throbbing head as she climbed off Santa's lap. When the room stopped spinning, she turned around to peek out the window then gasped, slapping her hands over her mouth.

Apparently, dressing up Mrs. C like a hooker, the elves like the Chippendales, and giving Santa a lap dance hadn't been enough while under the spell of the All Powerful Peppermintini. She'd strung a line of those damn glow in the dark festive Christmas condoms from one side to the other. She studied the shoppers outside the window. Shocked wasn't a strong enough word to describe the slack jaws, gaping pie holes, and bugged-out eyes staring back at her.

"Merry Christmas," Samantha said, as she clutched Mrs. C's coat tighter, smiled weakly, and waved.

"Jesus, Mary and Joseph what was Mr. Snow thinking?" a middle-aged man with a top hat said as he made the sign of the cross and patted his gasping wife.

"Well, he won't get my vote with a display like that." A woman with a pointy nose stuck up in the air tsked as she covered her daughter's eyes.

"Mrs. Claus has never looked so good if you ask me," said a leering old coot with tobacco-stained teeth.

Samantha wondered whom this Mr. Snow character was and what he could possibly have to do with Mark's shop. Feeling like an idiot, she stood there with her bed-head hair and baggy Christmas digs, no doubt looking like the star of a really bad porno. If only she hadn't fallen asleep.

She gnawed at her bottom lip and strove to find a way out of this mess, when a new spectator walked up to the window.

Samantha gasped. Tall, Dark and Stuffy? What on earth was he doing here?

She couldn't believe the same man from the bar last night stood outside of Mark's store this morning. Of all the bizarre coincidences, she thought. His eyes landed on her and sprang wide, then they narrowed in a dangerous scary way as they roamed around the storefront window.

Great. He truly must think she was certifiable.

"Interesting display, Mr. Snow," another shopper said.

He was Mr. Snow? This just kept getting better and better.

In the light of day, he looked even more stunning than he had the night before and still oddly familiar. He had black slicked back hair, black eyes, black clothes...and a black scowl to match. Not a pretty boy Ken doll attractive, but a brooding, macho, powerful kind of attractive with hard chiseled features more like Ken's evil brother, the devil himself.

Samantha found it hard to breathe.

He stepped aside as a petite, silver-haired pit-bull of a woman pulled out a set of keys and charged forward to slide the key in a lock...the same lock Samantha had jimmied the night before. Just peachy. He must work for Mark, along with Ms. Pit. Mr. Snow followed Ms. Pit inside, followed by half the town.

"You're probably wondering what I'm doing here," Samantha managed to say to Ms. Pit, while taking a wobbly step back from Stuffy's intimidating figure.

"Ya think!" Ms. Pit roared, while Stuffy stood there with a hard edge to his features.

Samantha grabbed her head and winced.

A light dawned in the small dynamo's beady eyes. "Not feeling so clever this morning, are we?" she asked in an even louder voice. "Serves you right," she added, flicking on all the bright lights she could find and opening the blinds fully.

Evil woman! Samantha shook off a wave of nausea. "Where's Mark and the hussy?" she ground out and looked past them both, searching the growing crowd.

Ms. Pit's gaze followed hers. "What are you blubbering about?"

"Your bosses. The owners. Where are they? I'd really like to go before they get here." Samantha stepped toward the door.

Tall, Dark and Stuffy blocked her path and spoke for the first time. The deep timber of his voice sent chills throughout Samantha's body that had nothing to do with the weather. "You aren't going anywhere except jail."

"J-Jail," she squeaked, her eyes colliding with his. What say did he have? He was just an employee. If anyone had pull, it would be Ms. Pitt. Ignoring Scary, she tried to appeal to the feminine side of the pit-bull...if there was one. "If you know the owner, then you should understand. He's a real ass."

Ms. Pit's face turned the color of beets, and she looked ready to explode. Before she could answer, those dark intense eyes of Scary's formed eerie slits. "You don't say." He crossed his arms over his sculpted chest. "It just so happens I do know the owner."

"Oh. Sounds like you like the guy." Probably because he *was* a guy, and well, Ms. Pitt had obviously embraced her "inner" guy. Samantha's heart plummeted right down to her stilettos. "Guess there's no chance you'd take my side then, huh." She wrung her hands in Mrs. C's threads.

"Not likely...considering *I'm* the 'real ass.'"

"Wait a minute." Samantha's brow knitted as she attempted

to clear the fog of her 'Tini hangover. "Isn't this Stowe's Boutiques?"

He arched a sleek black brow. "No. Stowe's Boutiques is two towns over. You're in Redemption, Massachusetts, and this is Snow's Antiques. I'm Nathan Snow."

Total shock followed by full-blown panic seized every cell in Samantha's body. When she finally picked her jaw up off the floor, she said in barely more than a whisper, "And I'm Samantha Darling, the biggest idiot of them all."

CHAPTER 2

THE NATHAN SNOW?

How could she not have recognized him? Apparently her subconscious had, because that's the name she'd slurred off the night before. Bile hit her throat. He was on all the covers of the business and entertainment magazines, listed as one of the wealthiest men in the Northeast, and one of the most eligible bachelors. Of all the shops to ransack, she had to choose one owned by a man with such a cold and ruthless reputation. She fell back on Santa's lap in a state of shock.

Ms. Pit shrieked, "Don't sit there, you imbecile! Go and 'carefully' change out of Mrs. Claus's clothes. Those are vintage antiques. They cost a fortune, and I'd like to try to salvage the material before you ruin them completely."

"Sorry. I had no idea." Samantha struggled to get up.

When she couldn't, Nathan reached out a large, masculine hand and helped her to her feet.

"Thanks," she said.

"I'd say it's my pleasure, but I'd be lying."

"Guess I deserved that." She wobbled over to Mrs. C and started to undress her, but Nathan stilled her.

"Allow my manager." He grunted. "I insist. You've done enough damage for one day."

Samantha stood there while Ms. Pit removed her bra, thong and garters from Mrs. C. She handed them to Samantha and pointed the way to the bathroom. So much for closure. Samantha had a feeling this new chapter in her life had only just begun.

Five minutes later, she emerged from the bathroom and handed Nathan Mrs. C's clothes. While Ms. Pit redressed Mrs. C and the elves, Nathan told the town's people to go, except for the judge and the sheriff who remained with Ms. Pit in case Nathan needed them. Nathan guided Samantha into his office. She sat down while he towered above her, and she told him her whole sappy story.

"This is what I propose," he said at last. "I won't have you arrested," she started to say thank you, relieved, but he held up a hand, "for now. It's Christmas, and contrary to popular belief, I'm not a Scrooge. Just because I don't like Christmas, doesn't mean I don't have a heart."

"How can you not like Christmas?" She gaped at him.

"That's neither here nor there," he responded. "The point is I have a business to run. Winning the Best Christmas Window Display contest brings a lot of shoppers into the winner's store. More shoppers means more business. I'm sick of Nancy's Knickknacks beating me every year."

His eyes took on a challenging gleam. "I come back to Redemption for the holidays every year specifically for this contest. This is where it all began for me, yet I have never won. This was supposed to be my year, but now I have to start all over. You come up with a winning display by Christmas Eve, and I won't press charges."

This was the greatest of all holidays. Surely, he would understand. "I'm not a drinker. Whatever was in that peppermint martini must have made me lose my mind, because I am not a girl who commits crimes. I will do whatever to make this up to you...but I always go home for Christmas a week early. This is *my* year to put the star on top of the tree. There has to be something we can work out."

"You sure this isn't about payback because I shot you down last night? Maybe you figured out who I was, looked me up, and took out your revenge." He leaned in until his face hovered only a few inches above hers. "Or maybe you were trying to finish what you started last night."

"I am *not* that kind of girl."

"Right." His gaze traced her features. "That's why you openly flirted with me from across the bar."

"I did not flirt. My well-meaning, idiot friends did. I am *never* spontaneous."

"You're saying what you did to my display was premeditated?"

"Of course not!" She ducked under his arm and stood, her heart imitating the little drummer boy.

"I've never seen some of the positions those elves were in." He stalked her like a predator, backing her up against his office wall. "I must admit what they were doing to Mrs. Claus was damn creative. Looked like it took a lot of thought."

"It took a lot of liquor," she squeaked, trying to find a way to escape. "No rational thoughts involved," she added, more to remind herself her dreams of the two of them reenacting those positions all night long had been completely irrational as well. "I was someone I don't even recognize."

"Oh, I recognize her. I've seen her kind before."

"I'm sure you have." She'd read all about his reputation, but she had no intention of becoming another notch on his belt. "I can assure you, she's long gone."

"Now you're a tease?"

"What do you expect me to say, let's do it right now? Fine, then." She thrust her chin up a notch. "Strip."

"As you wish." He loosened his tie, pulled it off and then undid the top button of his black silk shirt.

"I was joking!"

"I'm not." He undid the second button, letting the rest of the buttons slide out of the holes. His dress shirt fell open, revealing a fine sprinkling of hair beneath his undershirt. He slid his hand beneath the hem and lifted it above a tanned set of six pack abs.

"L-Look." Samantha tried not to stare as he released the T-shirt and shrugged broad shoulders out of the sleeves of his dress shirt. "I'm not a tease, and I'm not a prude. I'm just not...her."

Nathan finally took a step back, releasing his hold on her. He went to a wardrobe closet and pulled out a cashmere sweater—in black, of course—then slipped it over his head, the muscles in his wide back flexing and contracting with each movement. He dropped his silk shirt in a basket that read dry cleaning for Roz.

"That's a shame you're not her, but you still have to pay for her crimes."

"I will just as soon as the holidays are over."

"Sorry. *You* should have thought of that before you broke

into my shop." His face turned hard and unreadable. "You can go home on Christmas Eve so long as I win the contest."

He had every right to be mad at her, but she couldn't get over his unwillingness to compromise and his hot and cold behavior. "Wow, you really are a Scrooge," slipped out before she could stop it. "Don't you spend Christmas with anyone?"

His face darkened. "Wally, you can read Ms. Darling her rights," he hollered into the store. "Looks like she's choosing jail."

"Wait," she yelped. "I said you were a Scrooge. I didn't say I was stupid. I'll stay and create a display even grumpy you will like. Redemption can't be worse than jail."

He shrugged. "That remains to be seen."

"One week." She squared her shoulders.

Nathan nodded. "Think you can handle it?"

"In my sleep."

A spark of something flashed in his eyes, and his lips tipped up slightly.

"Aha!" She pointed at him.

"Aha what?" His brow puckered.

"Your face isn't made of granite after all."

Nathan spun on his heel, holding his watch up as he stormed out. "Clock's ticking, Ms. Darling."

"Ho, ho, flipping, ho, McScroogy. I'm on it."

Ms. Pit poked her silver head in, gave Samantha a nasty look, and slammed the door hard. Samantha grabbed her scalp on a moan. She might have a sentence to serve, but that didn't mean she couldn't serve it with the biggest dose of Christmas cheer they'd ever seen.

Determination overtook her. Yes indeedy, nice was safe,

and naughty was highly overrated, but taking Nathan Snow down a peg was beginning to sound oh so merry.

* * *

NATHAN HAD SENT his driver to Samantha's apartment to pick up some of the things she'd had her friends pack for her. Amber and Ellen sounded like quite a pair after the conversation he'd overheard. He refused to feel guilty. Samantha needed to be taught a lesson after what she'd done, but he had to admit she amused him. A plus this time of year. He hated the holidays.

Forcing those negative thoughts aside, he fought back a grin as he opened the door to the storage room. "Home sweet home."

Samantha stepped past him and jerked to a stop, the beige cotton trousers she'd changed into hugging her curvaceous backside. She'd twisted her sexy blond curls into a fancy professional knot at the back of her head again, but he'd seen her in action. She wasn't nearly as prim and proper as she let on, and he'd never been able to resist a challenge.

"This is *not* a bedroom?" She faced him with a horrified look on her heart-shaped face, her pale blue eyes wide and wary.

"There's a bed."

"A cot," she clarified.

"And a bathroom."

"An open toilet," her voice rose an octave, her cheeks turning the same shade of pink as her sweater.

"Be glad for four walls instead of bars of steel."

"You mean sheetrock and wires. There's no carpet, not

even a curtain. I'm grateful you didn't press charges, but you can't be serious."

"It's a work in progress, and I'm dead serious. I want to keep a close eye on you." He let his gaze run down the length of her and back up again. "Or there's always my place."

"I'll take my chances with the rats." She smirked.

He chuckled. If he made things difficult for her, she'd be desperate for his help. He'd help her into his bed, which is exactly where she wanted to be, whether she admitted it or not. He'd satisfy her obviously repressed desire, and maybe Christmas wouldn't be as lonely this year.

"You'll be fine." He left, whistling a lively tune, then called over his shoulder, "You've got work to do, Ms. Darling, and you can start by cleaning up your mess."

"Yes, sir," she snapped.

Yes, indeed, he thought on a full grin. Maybe this Christmas wouldn't be so bad after all.

* * *

THIS WAS TURNING out to be the worst Christmas ever. Samantha had spent hours cleaning up the mess she'd made and coming up with a new display. The window was closed off by room divider panels, and so far, Ms. Pit—the infamous dry-cleaning Roz—had left her alone. Nathan kept checking up on Samantha. Never knowing when he would poke his head in was driving her crazy. Trying to get a man who hated Christmas to like her ideas was nearly impossible.

"I don't like it," Nathan said yet again.

"Now, there's a big surprise," she grumbled, trying not to grind her teeth. "What don't you like this time?"

"I don't know, it looks...sparse. Maybe it needs more presents under the tree." He stood with his hands on his hips, tipping his head and studying the tree from various angles.

"You've got to be kidding. That's more than I ever got as a kid."

He stroked his heavy five o'clock shadow. "Seriously?" He looked genuinely surprised.

"The spirit of Christmas is not about how many presents you have under the tree."

"I knew that." He frowned, and she suspected he didn't know any such thing. "A light dawned in his eyes, and he held up a finger. "I've got it. Maybe we don't need more gifts, maybe we need *nicer* gifts. Or bigger ones. I wouldn't want the town to think I was cheap."

She threw her hands up. "I'm positive the town knows you're not cheap. You drive a BMW and wear a Rolex."

He went on as though not hearing her at all. "The tree is all wrong. You took off half my ornaments."

"You have an artificial monstrosity with enough ornaments to decorate the massive beauty in Rockefeller Center. There's no rhyme or reason to it. Your trimmings are all black and white, yet your ornaments are priceless antiques. Mr. and Mrs. C and the elves suggest an old fashion Christmas. I'd go for a more traditional approach."

"I happen to like modern."

"Said the antique store owner."

"You know what I mean."

"Apparently not." She tapped her foot to the beat of her rapidly rising pulse.

He lifted a shoulder. "I just want this store to succeed. I have my reasons."

Her foot stilled. "They really did a number on you."

A deep V formed on his forehead. "Who?"

"Your parents."

"You don't know what you're talking about." His features turned to granite.

Samantha gentled her tone. "Christmas is about the spirit of giving, not how much you can get. People know you have beautiful things. The reason they don't shop here is because you never *give* anything. Not a discount. Not even a smile. I hate to say it, but you're not very pleasant to be around."

His gaze pierced hers, and a chill froze her in place. "You've got spunk, Ms. Darling."

She straightened her spine. "I don't intimidate easily, Mr. Snow."

"I can see that." The corner of his mouth twitched. "But life isn't always pleasant. I don't have time to worry about what others think. We can't all be gobs of twinkling tinsel," he muttered, and his voice lowered as he repeated for the millionth time, "I'm not a Scrooge."

"You aren't jolly ole St. Nick, either." *That* was for sure. "I know all about life not being pleasant, but I am through wallowing in self-pity. Maybe you should do the same. If you want this particular store to improve, then winning this contest isn't enough. You need a plan."

"I take it you have something in mind?"

"I might have an idea, but it involves you letting me be the top dog."

He hesitated a beat and then said, "By all means, Boss, the top's all yours."

CHAPTER 3

"YOU'RE INSUFFERABLE," Samantha said.

"I try."

"Do me a favor." She glared at him. "Don't."

He chuckled. "This store holds a sentimental value for me." His face softened. "It's my baby. Giving up on it is not an option. So, how do I get the people in this town to see me in a new light, oh fairy godmother?"

"Lose the sarcasm for one. And work on changing your image. Getting the town to see you differently."

"I'm not putting on forty pounds and growing a beard for anyone, Darling." He had the gall to wink at her.

"And I'm not giving you a lap dance, so don't even think about it," she blurted, then pressed her lips together.

"Excuse me?" He scrutinized her with a sexy, curious gleam in his eye.

"Never mind." She took a swig of water. "You were saying?"

"Maybe we'd better take a break," he said. "Let's talk more over lunch."

"Deal." She held out her hand, and he slid his palm against hers. A jolt of desire snaked up her arm and slithered its way straight to her libido, making her acutely aware of just how long it had been.

Way too long, apparently.

* * *

"WE'RE DOING WHAT?" Nathan stared down at his designer pants and genuine Italian leather shoes.

Samantha was dressed like a snow bunny in her lavender ski jacket and matching boots. The woman was crazy, yet the most intriguing woman he'd ever met.

"We're cutting down a real tree," she answered.

"I already have a tree."

"That is *not* a tree."

"Then we can buy one."

She touched her finger to his lips. "Trust me, remember?"

He grunted. He'd learned the hard way the only person he could count on was himself. But he had to admit, she was entertaining. "I don't own a pair of jeans."

"There's a thrift store at the end of Main Street."

He had an image to project: one of stature, wealth and power. "There's no way I'm—"

"Trust involves no questions."

He recognized her stubborn streak and knew when to choose his battles. He'd save his demands for more important matters like convincing her his bed was where she needed to be. "Okay, but I want to be involved in all aspects. I always design my window myself."

"And that, my friend, is why you always lose." She laughed at the shocked expression he couldn't hide fast enough.

His mouth quirked at the sound of her laugh. Genuine. "You're not afraid to tell me exactly what you're thinking, unlike most people."

"I'd rather hear the truth than be blindsided any day."

He brushed a pale blond curl off her forehead and pulled up her faux fur trimmed hood, his desire to touch her outweighing his common sense. "Guess I'm not the only one who's been wounded."

She stiffened, pulling away. "You're not the only one who doesn't like to talk about it, either."

"Touché. If I'm to trust you, then you'll have to trust me. I need you to accompany me to some functions in the city."

"I thought you were home for the holidays on vacation."

"The truth is I'm married."

Her jaw fell open on a horrified expression, and he laughed a hearty laugh this time. She was such a refreshing change, that he couldn't help but tease her a bit. "I'm just being honest," he pointed out.

"So, where's this wife of yours?" she asked, not quite meeting his eyes.

"Wives," he corrected, thoroughly enjoying the way her cheeks flushed.

"Y-You're a polygamist?"

"My wives are not women. They're all ten of my stores. I can admit it because this is the life I chose. I'm happily married to my job. Taking a vacation never completely happens."

She relaxed. "What do you need me for?"

"There are a couple charity functions I need a date for."

"A d-date?" she stammered, back to blushing even brighter. "And you want to take me?"

Nathan paused on the words 'take me,' thinking she had no idea the extent of what he wanted to do with and to her. This time of year was the loneliest for him, memories of his child-hood depressing him. Seducing Samantha would be just the distraction he needed, but he didn't want a relationship. He had to be sure she was clear on that before he proceeded further, but make no mistake...

He *would* have her.

For now, he said, "Why not? I need a date, and you need to run your ideas by me."

"A business date." She looked both relieved and disap-pointed, and Nathan had to fight back a chuckle. "That makes sense."

"Good." He let his gaze bore into hers. "I usually get what I want."

"And that, my friend, is another thing we need to work on." She rolled her eyes. "Your arrogant attitude."

"Moi? Arrogant? Never." His lips twitched.

"You're hopeless." She laughed again, the tinkling sound filling him with a sensation he couldn't remember the last time he'd felt: joy.

"And you, *my friend*, are a most interesting woman." Her mouth parted like she wanted to say something, but he touched his finger to her lips like she had him. "Later, Ms. Darling. It's getting late."

"That's right, and we still have a tree to cut down."

"Not so fast." Nathan grabbed her arm. "Tomorrow will be soon enough to start phase one of your plan." His voice turned husky. "You can be the boss during the day, but I get to be the boss at night. According to my watch, it's officially night. I get to call the shots, and you have to do everything I tell you to...no questions asked." His words were innocent, but he knew his eyes were filled with pure sin.

"Oh, well, I'm not so sure that's a good—"

He stilled her words when he cradled her cheeks with his palms. "Trust me," he murmured softly.

"I trust you." She licked her lips, and his eyes zeroed in, making his own lips burn to press against hers. As she pulled away, he could have sworn he heard her mumble something about trusting herself was another matter entirely.

"I'll pick you up at seven," he said to her hastily retreating back.

Her hand waved in the air, but she didn't say a word.

* * *

"Wow." Nathan stared in awe at the vision of loveliness standing before him. "You look beautiful."

"Thank you." A becoming shade of pink tinted Samantha's cheeks. She smoothed her hands down the front of her ruby red chiffon dress, discreetly tugging the snug material down further over her curvy hips. It kept riding up above her knees, revealing more of her spectacular legs. "Told you I like to eat." She laughed, sounding nervous. "One too many Christmas cookies, I guess."

"You look amazing." He meant every word as he held out the arm of his black Armani tuxedo. "Shall we?"

Tonight's charity dinner in Boston was ten thousand dollars a plate. Homes for the Children had always been a cause he'd felt strongly about. He might have grown up with everything, but he'd always felt alone. Snow's Antiques was the biggest contributor every year. Nathan made sure of it. The money they raised tonight would keep the orphanages in the greater Boston area going all year.

"Hey, you in there?" Samantha touched his hand.

He smiled down at her as he led her to the waiting limo. "Just thinking about how much fun we're going to have tonight."

"I thought these shindigs were boring."

"When you're with the right person, it doesn't matter where you are. And," once they were seated, he handed her a glass of Champagne, "they have a dance floor."

"I am never touching that poison again, and I can't dance."

He replaced her champagne with a bottle of Perrier. "I can."

"That's hardly fair."

"Sue me." He sipped his champagne, deciding Cristal was his new favorite.

"Maybe I will." She downed half her bottle.

"For what?"

"Breach of contract. This dancing stuff wasn't part of the deal."

He paused as he considered his argument. "You're the one who agreed to let me be the boss at night, and you're the one who came up with the 'trust me' with no questions asked rule. You brought this upon yourself, Darling."

Her lips pursed in an adorable pout. "Don't blame me when we look like contestants auditioning for 'America's got Diddly' out there."

"I'm a great teacher."

"If you say so." She shook her head, and a couple of blond strands slipped loose to frame her face in soft ringlets.

"There are a lot of things I'd like to teach you. Dancing is only the beginning." His eyes heated, and he watched her skin quiver as though he'd physically touched her.

She inhaled a deep breath, and her face flushed a becoming shade of rose. "I'm not sure—"

"We're here." He opened the door and slid out. She'd come around. He'd see to it. He always got what he wanted, and right now, he wanted her...

Undressed and in his bed with no questions asked.

He opened her door and held out his hand. "Shall we?"

SAMANTHA STUDIED NATHAN. His expensive tuxedo was all black and tailored perfectly. His slicked back hair made him look fierce and powerful. His armor, so to speak, that let everyone know he was ruthless and not to be taken for granted. Even though she was dying to mess him up, she had to admit this style gave him a dangerous quality that appealed to her inner vixen.

If he only knew her inner thoughts, he'd be shocked. No matter how much she might want him, she'd read enough about him in the tabloids. He was a ladies' man, but had never been in a serious relationship. Getting involved with him had major heartache written all over it.

He knew exactly what he did to her, but two could play at this game, she thought, deciding to make him squirm for a change. She had to make him realize he wasn't in control, before she did something stupid. She didn't plan to follow through on her seduction, simply let him see what it felt like to want someone so badly but not be able to have them. She smiled slightly, a little thrill coursing through her at the thought.

"What's that look for," he asked from their table near the dance floor.

"Just deciding you were right. Tonight is most definitely going to be fun." She grabbed a goblet of water off the table and took a sip, looking around.

Soft lighting, crystal chandeliers and silk tablecloths were only the beginning. A full piece orchestra occupied the entire corner on the opposite side of the dance floor. Politicians, entertainers, and business executives she'd seen plastered in the magazines and on the news moved across the dance floor in a waltz. And tantalizing aromas of foods she couldn't begin to name bathed the room in a heady swirl of bliss.

"Hard to get used to, I know," he broke into her thoughts.

"I can't believe you give so much to help these kids. That's amazing. I mean ten thousand dollars a plate is a lot of money."

"Well, one-hundred actually."

She choked on her drink. "You give one-hundred-thousand dollars? This charity must mean a lot to you." Maybe there was more to him than she first thought.

He shrugged, looking uncomfortable, then snagged another glass of champagne from a waiter's tray.

"Snow, you've done it again," Senator Perry said, stopping by their table. "I thought this year your old man might actually beat you, but somehow, you always manage to figure out what he'll give and top him. Well played, boy." He clinked his glass to Nathan's. "Maybe if he'd make an appearance for once, instead of jet setting all over the world, he'd fare better."

The Senator moved on to talk with a celebrity at another table, and Nathan conversed with various important people as Samantha watched and listened.

A smooth talking, well refined, yet distant enigma. She was usually a good judge of character, but she'd been way off when it came to Mark. It was a shame that Nathan's generosity stemmed from a need to outshine his father. She'd been right all along. He had no heart and was as cold and ruthless as they said.

"I know what you're thinking, but you're wrong," he said when they were alone again. "I grew up surrounded by such wealth and power, yet I've never been comfortable with it. Venturing out on my own, making my own money, making a name for myself...that was much more satisfying than being born into fame and fortune. At times I'm tempted to give it all away and start over again." He swirled the liquid in his glass, staring down into the gold contents. "Once you've achieved your goals, life gets boring."

He looked lonely, almost vulnerable. She wanted to hug him and tell him it would be all right. "Maybe starting over isn't what you need," she said. "Maybe adding a family is the void you're trying to fill." Oops, had she said that out loud?

His gaze snapped to her eyes, locked, and held. "I told you...I'm already married."

"Right." She licked her lips, remembering her mission to make him suffer like she was and to gain a bit of control back. She kicked off her shoes. "Maybe there's another void you're thinking of filling, then." She slipped her bare foot under the edge of his pant leg until her toes touched the warm skin of his shin above his dress sock.

"Careful, Ms. Darling," his voice growled. "You're playing

with fire."

"It's okay," she said in a voice that sounded breathy to her own ears. "I know how to stop, drop and roll." She couldn't believe the things that were coming out of her mouth, but he'd been driving her crazy for days, and turnabout was fair play.

"Dance with me," he said. It wasn't a question. He pulled her to her feet before she could come up with a fathomable protest. The next thing she knew, she was in his arms, held tenderly as he framed her with all his godliness.

He pressed his palm to the small of her bare back and moved her seamlessly around the dance floor. She stumbled, but he quickly pressed her tight against him. Her bulging cleavage flattened against the contours of his rock-solid pectoral muscles, yet he continued to move without missing a beat.

She, on the other hand, couldn't inhale enough air.

"I thought our bodies weren't supposed to touch in a waltz?" She asked, swallowing hard, trying not to feel the play of his chest and thigh muscles as they moved beneath the fine material of his tuxedo, or the hard bulge of what was nestled against her. Mission accomplished. She'd definitely affected him. Glancing around, she tried to see if anyone was watching her, but no one paid them any attention. Obviously, she wasn't the first woman they'd seen him with in a precarious position.

"I don't give a damn what anyone thinks, Ms. Darling," he stated, as though reading her mind. "Certain situations call for a different technique. I wouldn't want you to fall," he whispered seductively close to her ear, his warm breath tickling the hairs on her neck.

He smelled amazing. She leaned back and looked at him hungrily. "I can assure you, Mr. Snow, I have no intention of falling."

He nodded once; his eyes boring into hers. "Good. Then we're on the same page." His voice lowered to a husky decibel. "Because falling wouldn't be good for your well-being."

"E-Exactly." She nodded back, glad he understood she had no intention of taking this dance of flirtation any further than the dance floor. "Well, thank you." She tried to step out of his embrace. "You're—"

"Not done." He tightened his arms around her. His head swooped down and mouth covered hers, his tongue plunging deep to mate with her own.

Stars exploded behind her eyes, and waves of heat rolled over her, sprinkling her skin with tiny prickly bumps. His cologne smelled expensive mixed with a spellbinding manly fragrance that was pure Nathan. And his heavily whiskered face felt rough yet thrilling against hers as his mouth worked magic.

She couldn't see, couldn't think, couldn't do anything but feel, and a desire more powerful than anything she'd ever experienced ripped through her. Her knees caved, but she never hit the floor. Strong arms tightened, pressing her firmly against a solid wall of muscle, and her arms wrapped around his neck to hold on for dear life. After what felt like an eternity of sheer ecstasy, Nathan finally broke the kiss and set her down.

He stepped back and winked. "Told you I wouldn't let you fall."

She just blinked at him, speechless, terrified it may already be too late.

CHAPTER 4

THE NEXT MORNING, Samantha decided to put any thoughts of intimacy with Nathan out of her mind. But no matter how hard she tried, she couldn't stop reliving that amazing kiss.

Nathan strolled out of Betty's Thrift Store and joined Samantha in front of Sal's Hardware. While he'd always looked sharp in his designer pants and tailor-made shirts, Samantha decided he looked hot in a pair of snug fitting jeans and a soft burgundy sweater. His hair lay in soft, pomade-free black waves, making his olive skin and permanent five-o'clock shadow look even sexier and more approachable.

Nancy of Nancy's Knickknacks strolled out of her shop and smirked at Nathan as though he didn't stand a chance again this year. But Samantha didn't miss the look of longing that had passed over Nancy's face when she'd first spotted him. A surge of something Samantha wasn't ready to identify swept through her, but she shrugged it off as indigestion.

"I look stupid," he said.

"You look hot."

One corner of his lips hitched up, making her ears burn.

"I mean, you look fine, but you must be hot in that thick sweater."

He smiled fully, now. "I'm not wearing a coat, so I'm okay. The question is how are you?"

"No questions. Trust me, remember?"

"I trust you think I'm hot."

"And I trust you need more help than I thought, Mr. Snow."

"Call me Nathan. It's silly to be so formal, given how you feel about me." His eyes twinkled.

"You really are arrogant." Samantha shook her head. "I do agree being so formal—when you *did* ask me out on a date—is silly. Call me Samantha."

His eyes smoldered at the word date, and she tried to clarify she was kidding, but he cut her off. "I'm honored, Samantha."

He brought her hand to his lips and kissed her palm. His hot breath fanned over her nerve endings, sending her pulse into a double-time rendition of, "Fa la la la laaa, la la la laaa."

"From rambling to speechless," his deep voice rumbled low and delicious. "Remarkable. Maybe this week won't be as painful as I imagined."

"Humph!" Samantha yanked her hand from his. "Let's go, Snow. Clock's ticking."

She held up her wrist and tapped her much cheaper watch, as she marched into the hardware store to buy a saw with Nathan laughing all the way.

* * *

TWO HOURS later Nathan sounded frustrated. "How about this one?"

Samantha walked around the tree, not willing to quit until she was satisfied. "No."

"Why?"

"It's got a big hole in the back."

"No one will see it."

"I'll know it's there."

He sighed. "Fine." He kept walking until he came to a stop in front of another tree. After mimicking her actions, he said, "This one doesn't have a single hole." He pulled out the saw.

"No."

"What's the problem this time?"

"It's too fat."

He grunted. "Only a woman could get away with saying something like that."

"Funny. It will take up too much room."

He rolled his head, then started walking again. He came to a stop in front of yet another tree and circled it. "This one is perfect. No holes and nice and skinny."

"Too skinny."

"I thought there was no such thing as too skinny?"

"Do I look like I'm into skinny?" Samantha enjoyed a little thing called eating to ever be a model, even though she'd been told she had Barbie doll looks since she'd hit puberty.

His gaze ran over her, stopping to linger on all the right curves. "You look damn near perfect to me."

"I do?" The very air around them charged with sizzling sexual tension.

He cleared his throat and started walking again. "I'm not much of an outdoors man, and frankly, never cared to be."

A short time later, Samantha let out a squeal and grabbed his arm. "Oh, my God."

"What? A bear, a wolf, what do you see?" He shoved her behind him and wielded the saw as though it was a sword.

Her heart melted as she responded, "The perfect tree, but feel free to kill the beast. It does have fur, after all." She pointed to the perfect Douglas Fir before them and tried not to giggle.

He lowered his arm and gaped at her. "The perfect tree?"

"I always get excited when I find the perfect tree. This is going to look amazing."

He circled the tree in what had now become a ritual, then plopped his hands on his hips. "I'm just glad to be done." He dropped down on his hands and knees, struggled for a minute until he got the hang of the saw, then successfully cut down the tree. He stood up and wiped his brow, wearing a huge grin and a smudge of dirt. "Not bad for a guy who never had to do a chore a day in his life."

"Wow, that must have been rough," she said dryly.

"I might not have had to work and got anything I wanted, but I never saw much of my parents then." He dusted the dirt off his knees, his smile all but gone. "Still don't now."

"Nathan, I'm sorry." She couldn't resist cupping his cheek with her palm.

He squeezed her hand before she could pull away, like he hadn't received nearly enough affection in life. "Don't be. At least I learned one thing from being raised by them."

"What's that?"

"How to appreciate the finer things in life." He winked, his smile returning as he studied his handiwork. "What now, Boss?"

"We drag it out of the woods and tie it to the top of your car."

His smile vanished. "Like hell."

She shot him a look of disapproval.

He grunted. "I'll make you a deal. I'll drag that 'thing' God knows how many miles back to my car, but no way am I tying it to my Beamer."

"Fair enough."

"I CAN'T BELIEVE I'm going to admit this, but you were right. The tree is perfect," Nathan said the next morning after breakfast.

"Excuse me?" Samantha sipped her coffee with glee. They'd uncovered the window to see the tree in the light of day.

"You heard me," he said, running a hand through his still gel-free hair and his sweater was a deep green today instead of his trademark black. "I'm just glad we got it here."

"The look on the tow-truck driver's face when he showed up expecting to tow your car only to wind up towing your Christmas tree was priceless."

"I paid him the full amount and a hefty tip for very little work. He should be thanking me."

"And you should be thanking me."

"I'll give you that." Nathan sipped his coffee, studying her over the rim of his cup, looking adorable. He wasn't nearly as cold and ruthless as he let everyone believe. "What's next, Boss?"

"We make our decorations."

His brows shot up. "*Make* them?"

"It'll be fun. You'll see."

"I don't have a crafty bone in my body."

"Old fashioned, traditional Christmas. Trust me, okay?"

He scrubbed a hand over his face. "Whatever you say."

"I say we start at Bob's craft store."

"Win over another small business owner by shopping in his store while creating a display with heart," Nathan said more to himself, thinking aloud. "Two birds with one stone. You're smarter than you look, Darling."

"Thanks, I think." She set her cup on the mantel of the fireplace. "Let's get to work."

They shopped at Bob's and then talked and laughed while they worked all morning, until someone knocked on the front window, startling them both. They'd forgotten to recover the window in their craft making frenzy. They had already strung popcorn and cranberry garland, created hand painted paper machete ornaments, and made sparkly tinsel, then they hung them on the tree. All that was left was the star on the top and plugging in the lights.

Sal, Betty and Bob stood waving outside.

Since they were here, they might as well give them a sneak peak before recovering the window. "Want to do the honors," Samantha said.

"You sure?" Nathan questioned.

"Absolutely. This is your tree. You should be the one to put the star on the top."

"Okay, but I've never done this before."

Her eyes grew misty. Poor guy had never experienced a "real" Christmas.

"You okay?" he asked.

"I'm fine. Do me proud."

He grinned wide then stood tall and graced the top of the tree with a star he had made with his own two hands out of wire and glittering tinfoil. If that wasn't heart, then she didn't know what was.

"It's perfect," she said, thinking he was perfect...and she was in big trouble.

"You done good, Boss." He glanced out the window only to receive the thumbs-up sign.

"Looks like your fellow Redemption business owners are starting to warm up to you."

Nathan waved back. "Thanks to you, but they're not the ones who vote on the display."

"And that's where phase two comes into play."

"Phase two?" he asked in a wary voice.

She laughed. "It's not that bad. You just need to win over the local citizens."

"Why do I have a feeling I'm not going to like what you have in mind?"

"No questions, remember? Trust—"

"I got it, Boss. And for the record," his gaze softened as it met hers, "I do."

A warm glow wrapped itself around her heart. "Back to work," she said. "We have a lot to do before tomorrow."

"What's tomorrow?"

She winked and tried not to giggle. "You'll see."

"Fine, but just remember what they say about payback, and never forget...your nights are mine."

CHAPTER 5

"You big chicken." Samantha grabbed Nathan's hand and pulled him out the door the next day at dusk.

So many people had misjudged Nathan, including herself. They had no idea that beneath that cold, aloof, arrogant exterior beat the heart of a man who truly cared. The façade he put on was all for show. That way no one got close enough to hurt him. He wasn't so different from her. They just guarded their hearts in different ways.

"Where are we going?" he asked, wearing a bored expression, but she saw a glimmer of excitement.

"It's a surprise."

"Should I be afraid?" He arched a thick black brow as he stared down at her from his impressive height.

She grinned up at him. "No worries, McScroogy. I've got your back."

"How many times do I have to tell you I'm not a scrooge?" he said with much less bite this time.

She fluttered her eyelashes at him. "If the personality fits…"

He looked at her dryly. "If I were a scrooge, I wouldn't be here at all."

"True. I guess there's hope for you after all."

"Depends on what we're doing. You ever going to enlighten me?"

"Absolutely." She walked up the steps to a house. "You ready?"

He glanced at her with a puckered brow. "For what?"

She pushed the doorbell.

The door swung open, while a husband, his wife, and his three children looked at them curiously. Samantha jabbed him in the side with her elbow and help up a stack of papers before him. She started singing *Silent Night, Holy Night* in the best voice she could muster.

His jaw dropped open, but then he cleared his voice and started to sing along with her. He was right; payback really was fun because he couldn't sing a note. She tried not to wince as he struggled but never stopped singing. The husband and wife looked at him, smiled fondly and clapped louder than they needed to. Nathan bowed, but his face was redder than normal, and then he marched away with his hand on Samantha's back.

"Touché," he said when they were out of earshot.

"What do you mean?" she asked, feigning innocence

"I get it. Payback for making you dance."

"You don't get anything. This was about letting the towns-folk know you're human—vulnerable—just like the rest of us. They need to see you're not perfect."

"Trust me, Ms. Darling. I'm anything but perfect."

"Good," she responded softly. "Because, neither am I."

He took her hand and led her to the next house. "Then let's do this thing."

For the next hour, they sang for house after house until they reached the end of Main Street. The looks they received were wary, then surprised, then endearing. Nathan had no idea how much it meant for people to relate to him. To feel for him.

The snow fell in fat heavy flakes, the sky an inky black, and the air surrounding them grew still and silent. It felt like being in the middle of a snow globe. Nathan grabbed her hand and pulled her to a field past the dead-end road.

"What are you doing?"

He glanced at his watch. "It's officially night. I'm in charge."

She swallowed hard. "Oh. Well. What exactly do you have in mind?"

He grinned like a schoolboy. "Snow angels."

Her jaw unhinged, and she smiled right along with him. "Seriously?"

"Don't you know by now I'm the serious sort?"

"After today, I found you quite humorous."

"Did you, now?" He advanced on her, backing her up to the edge of the dead-end road.

"What are you doing?"

He didn't say a word, just kept stalking her.

"You're freaking me out."

"Welcome to how I felt when I realized I had to sing. Did I tell you I'm tone deaf?" His eyes narrowed with a look so intense and downright scary.

"What are you going to do to me? It's freezing. Way too cold to make snow angels."

"Trust me." He pounced, tackling her and rolling at the last second so she landed on top of him.

"I…" She stared down into eyes so dark and passionate and full of repressed emotions she couldn't resist stroking his cheeks.

"I know…me too," he responded, then rolled her over and covered her mouth with his own.

Warm full lips pressed hotly against hers, and every cell in her body came alive. When his tongue slipped between her lips, heat infused her system, warming her core and steaming out her pores. He tasted delicious. His kiss full of coffee and spice and sin all rolled into one mouth-watering morsel.

When he finally came up for air, she panted heavily. "What was that all about?"

"A friendly kiss to warm you up." He winked and rolled to his feet. "Let's go, Darling. That snow is way too tempting. Race ya." He jogged into the middle of the field where the snow was the freshest and deepest.

She took a deep breath, letting her heartbeat slow as she watched the muscles of his legs and gluts play beneath the material of his jeans and had to agree: *Snow* was about the most tempting thing she'd seen in a year, and that kiss had been a hell of a lot more than friendly. But what she feared the most was getting hurt by the frost he could bite her with.

WEDNESDAY MORNING DAWNED bright and sunny, the freshly fallen snow from the night before sparkling as though it was covered with millions of precious diamonds. There was nothing more magical than a white Christmas. Samantha and

Nathan had spent the night making snow angels, then stopping into Cindy's Café for hot chocolate.

Samantha knew he found her attractive, but he'd also made it perfectly clear he was married to his job. He wasn't looking for a relationship. She wasn't looking for a relationship, either. She was terrified of getting her heart broken again. Maybe her friends were right, and she needed to have an affair to get Mark out of her system for good. If she went into this knowing the expectations, then her heart should be safe. Except, she'd never been an affair type of girl.

Her mother always said food was the way to a man's heart, except Samantha couldn't cook. She knew exactly what they were going to do today. Bake Christmas cookies for the church bake sale. How hard could that be?

A knock sounded on her door. Smoothing the front of her pale pink clingy sweater that accented all of her curves, she took one last look at her reflection. Snug jeans, cute high-heeled boots, hair hanging free in soft curls, and the pink in her cheeks the perfect accessory. She opened the door and tried not to look nervous.

His gaze ran over her and an appreciative expression softened his hard chiseled features. She equally appreciated him in his black nylon warm-up pants and jacket. Dressy, sporty, or casual...he always looked amazing.

"What's on the agenda for today, Boss?" he asked.

"Cooking."

"What kind of cooking are we talking about?"

"Baking Christmas cookies for the church bake sale."

"Beauty and brains. You're amazing. Did anyone ever tell you that?"

"No, but feel free to any time the spirit moves you." She

patted his arm then led the way into the shop. "Let's see what we can do about scrounging up some baking supplies." She started rifling through cupboards and drawers.

"I know exactly where we can find the best," he said from behind her. When she turned around, he held out her coat.

She looked at him curiously as she took her jacket. "I'm sure you do. Let me guess, a high-end store on the other side of town?"

"On the other side of town, yes. I high-end store...not exactly. Follow me." He opened the door to the shop.

"Where to?" Samantha asked, as she trailed behind him.

"My place."

A thrill ran through her. "Okay."

He hesitated, looking surprised. "No argument?"

"Not a one," she said softly, then added, "I trust you."

"Oh-kay," he responded warily. "What's the catch?"

"No catch." She walked along beside him, surprised when he passed his car and opted to walk. "You've changed." She slipped her hand around his arm.

"Maybe, a little, but don't fool yourself into thinking I'm all warm and fuzzy like you." His words said one thing, but his actions spoke volumes as he bent his arm to secure her hand more tightly against him.

"McScroogy warm and fuzzy? Never. I just figure we're halfway to goal, and surprisingly, we work well together." She shrugged. "I'm curious to see how the other half lives. Besides, we're both adults, and the entire town knows I can't leave until my sentence is up. They'd know if I suddenly went missing so it's not like you can do anything to me."

His heavy-lidded gaze dropped to hers, and the heat from his eyes pooled in her midsection. "You think you know me, Samantha, but you have no idea what I'm capable of."

"Like what?" she asked breathlessly at the sound of her name on his lips, trying not to sound eager. Excited. But for the first time in a long time, that's exactly what she was.

He stopped, turned, pulled her into his arms and slowly lowered his head to hers. Her eyelids started to flutter closed in anticipation. As she parted her lips, he whispered in her ear, "I'm going to teach you how to make cookies."

"Huh?" Her eyes sprang open.

He chuckled as he stepped away to open the door to his townhouse.

Her eyebrows shot up. "This is where you live?"

He glanced over his shoulder. "*This* other half prefers to live modestly."

"But you must own several places." She followed him inside and shut the door.

"And they're all like this," he said matter-of-factly. "I prefer to spend my money on more important things than mansions. I leave those to people like my parents."

"I see," she said, kicking herself for putting the tension back in his voice. "I like modest," she added, following him through a decent sized living room with two bedrooms and a bathroom to the right, a dining room straight ahead, and a kitchen to the left.

"Thanks," he said, already pulling out pots and pans as though more than ready to change the topic.

"Love the antiques," she added.

"Thanks." He shot her a warm genuine smile that deepened the crow's feet at the corners of his eyes and made the butterflies dance in her belly. "Ready?"

"Oh, yeah." She bit her bottom lip, then frowned. "Um, wait. For what?"

"To get cooking. What did you think I was talking about?" he asked innocently.

"Nothing," she answered quickly but suspected he was playing with her.

"Bet I can make better cookies than you," he challenged.

Her grin came slow and sweet. "You're on."

"Are you hustling me, Darling?" He advanced on her, backing her up against the counter. "Last time I checked, that was naughty. I thought you were being nice these days."

"I can be very nice, just tell me what you'd like for me to do?" She licked her lips, feeling daring.

His gaze dropped to her lips, and he responded in a husky voice, "You're the boss. You tell me what to do. I'm good, remember?"

"Prove it," she dared him.

"Careful what you ask McScroogy for, Darling. You don't have to be nice for me to deliver."

"Deliver what?"

"You really want to go there?"

She opened her mouth to reply but then chickened out and said, "Yup, I want to go to the stove. We have cookies to bake, you slacker."

He blinked, but then a loud laugh burst out of his chest. "You amaze me, Darling."

"You ain't seen nothin' yet." She winked.

For the next hour, he proceeded to out bake her in every way imaginable.

"I'm not seeing much progress on your part other than making a mess." He wiped flour on the end of her nose.

"Hey." She swatted his hand away and swiped at his face, but he caught her wrist. "You're the one who hustled me."

He kissed the inside of her wrist. "It's not called hustling when I never said I couldn't cook."

"Well, it sure as heck is called something." She snorted.

He stared at her, not saying a word, but his body language screamed, *It's called foreplay, Darling*. She swallowed hard, knowing it was what she wanted, but not knowing how to make the first move. His lips tipped up in a full delicious lazy grin that said, *Allow me*. He hooked the front of her apron with his finger and started pulling her toward him. Her eyelids fluttered closed and she let out a soft sigh, awaiting the touch of his mouth to hers.

The smoke alarm screeched, ruining the moment as the kitchen filled with smoke. Nathan bolted to the stove, grabbing oven mitts along the way, and pulled out a sheet of charred cookies. Meanwhile, Samantha opened the window, snatched a towel, and started fanning the smoke detector. When the horrendous noise finally ceased, they looked at each other and laughed.

"Someone forgot to set the timer," she said.

"Someone was a bit distracted," he responded. "I believe we were in the middle of—"

"Finishing our cookies for the church bake sale. You're exactly right." She tried not to giggle at his you're-killing-me expression.

"Lucky me."

"You *are* lucky I've decided to help you." She bit her bottom lip and tried to swat him.

He caught her hand. "And *you* are lucky I've decided to be lenient and not punish you for being naughty." His gaze dropped to her mouth. "Keep biting that lip and I might change my mind."

"Oh?" she said.

"Oh, yeah," he responded.

"Oh, my. And what exactly did you have in mind?"

"Why don't I show you?" He stepped forward until he was a hair away from touching her, but he kept his hands by his sides. "First, I would—" His cell phone rang, and he cursed under his breath as he glanced at the caller ID. "It's Roz. Sorry, I have to take this."

"Go ahead." Samantha cleared her dry throat. "I have to get these cookies over to the bake sale early anyway, and I could use some fresh air. I'll meet you there tonight. You can show me whatever it was you intended to do later if you want."

"Make no mistake, Ms. Darling...I want." He gave her one last heated gaze and then walked away to answer his phone.

Samantha packed up the cookies that weren't burnt and headed out the door. Hot didn't begin to describe how she felt, and he hadn't even touched. She was pretty certain she would burst into flames after he was through punishing her...yet she'd never looked forward to anything more.

NATHAN SMOOTHED the front of his burnt orange cashmere sweater over his jeans. He'd never been a fan of jeans or color. Ever since Samantha had come into his life, he found himself wearing both on a daily basis. He could fool himself into thinking he only wore them to soften his image, but he knew the real reason.

Samantha.

He actually cared about what she thought of him. That was a first. He'd done a lot of firsts with her, and he wanted to do a whole lot more to her. His palms started to sweat with just the thought of how she'd made him feel earlier.

He never brought women home. He preferred to stay in a hotel or at their place. He might own several apartments and town houses, but each of them was his own personal space. A place to be himself and not let the world in. Women were meant to be cherished and pampered and adored...but never loved. He'd learned the hard way that when you let someone in and loved them, they let you down.

It concerned him that he'd let his guard down enough to bring Samantha back to his place, but then he reasoned this was different. She was working off her sentence and staying in the back of his store. Redemption's only hotel was run by the biggest busy body in town. His townhouse was the only suitable place for what he had planned: wooing Samantha Darling straight into his bed. After how she'd acted earlier, he was certain they were on the same page.

She probably played the game as well as he did.

He glanced around his place one more time. Everything was ready for his night of seduction. The wine was chilling on the table. The candles were ready to be lit. The music and lighting were set to the perfect level. He just needed the object of his desire, and he might stand of chance of forgetting what the holidays did to him.

He grabbed his keys and was just about to head out the door when his house phone rang. Frowning, he glanced at his watch. Everyone in town was already at the bake sale. Who could it be? A moment of dread filled him as he wondered if it could be his parents. He grudgingly made his way into his kitchen and looked at the caller ID. A number he didn't recognize.

"Nathan Snow residence, may I help you?"

"Wow, so formal," one woman said, sounding like she had him on speaker phone.

"Yeah, but Tall, Dark and Stuffy sounds just as yummy as we thought he would," another woman said, confirming the annoying speaker feature.

"Apparently you know who I am. Do me the courtesy of cluing me in as to who you both are."

"Whoops, sorry," they both said, followed by a few giggles.

"I'm Amber."

"And I'm Ellen."

"Ah, Ms. Darling's friends."

"Then you must know how much we care about her," the other woman who called herself Ellen said.

"Getting her drunk and trying to hook her up with me is a funny way of showing that."

"We would never do anything to hurt her," Amber said. "We just underestimated her alcohol tolerance."

"Brilliant observation," he said dryly. "What she did to Santa, Mrs. Claus and my elves was clearly coal worthy."

"What I think is you're a—"

"A really nice guy who didn't deserve the trouble she caused in her attempt to get back at her ex-fiancé Mark," Ellen quickly cut Amber off. "I get that she deserves to be punished," she went on, "but she doesn't deserve to have her favorite holiday ruined. You should let her go home in time for Christmas Eve. If you make her miss putting the star on the top of her family tree, she will be devastated. She's already had one man succeed in ruining it. Please don't add to that," she pleaded.

He hesitated, thinking about what they'd said, but then his selfish side emerged. He wasn't ready to let Samantha go, he admitted. Wrong or right, he wanted her, and he wouldn't set her free until he had her. "She's lucky I'm not having her arrested," he finally said. "As long as I win the contest, then she will be free to go on Christmas Eve night. If she drives fast enough, she just might make it home in time."

"Wow, you really are a mean one, Mr. Grinch," Amber said with a bitter tone.

"No, he's an ass," Ellen said, her good cop tone completely gone. "I think he's full of reindeer crap. I think it's all an act, and he does care, but he's too stubborn to admit it."

"Why is this contest so important to you, anyway?" Amber asked.

"I have my reasons." Nathan clenched his jaw, not letting the fact that they were right get to him.

"If those reasons include keeping Sam around long enough to seduce her, then you'd better re-evaluate, buddy. Karma's a bitch, and breaking her heart would not be good for your soul."

"I thought I didn't have a soul."

"Even the real Grinch had a heart, he just needed someone to knock some sense into him before he realized the consequences of his actions," Ellen said meaningfully. "Samantha might act like she would be into casual sex, but she is so warm-hearted and caring; she can't help but fall easily and fall hard."

"Somehow I don't think you want any strings," Amber

chimed in. "Trust me when I say seducing Samantha comes with a whole ball of yarn."

"Are we done here, ladies?"

"Honey, we're just getting started."

Well, hell....

CHAPTER 6

"Wow, that color green suits you," Samantha said to Nathan when he joined her in the lobby of Sacred Heart church, her gaze traveling over the tapered cashmere that hugged his impressive frame deliciously.

"Thank you." He kept his eyes locked on hers, never once venturing into the land of inappropriate, darnit. "I must say you look lovely in green velvet."

"Thank you." Something was off. This afternoon he'd been more than ready to heat things up. What the hell had happened between then and now? "Nathan, I—"

"Ms. Darling, you must give me the recipe for these gingerbread cookies. They are divine," Betty said, stepping in between them.

"That was all Mr. Snow's doing. You'll have to ask him."

She blinked, her owl eyes going wide. "You don't say." She turned to focus on Nathan, who stood looking vastly uncomfortable. "You are one surprising man, Mr. Snow."

He recovered quickly and turned on a charm Samantha

didn't know he possessed. "Thank you, ma'am, and please call me Nathan."

"Only if you call me Betty." She winked.

"It would be my pleasure, Betty. And might I say I've grown rather fond of the jeans you carry in your thrift store."

"Oh, go on with you, now." Her hands fluttered about.

"Whatever the heck these doohickies are, they're delicious," Sal said, as he joined them.

"They're called Fattigmann, and you're probably tasting the figs I used," Nathan said.

Sal's eyes bulged. "*You* made these?" he sputtered. "I thought Miss Darling did."

"I made the sugar cookies on the end of the table." She pointed to the mess she'd attempted to decorate, which ended up looking like a kindergarten project, and tried not to blush.

"Do I ever," Sal said in wonder, his forehead wrinkling in disbelief. "How did you find the time, Mr. Snow?"

"Thanks to you and the saw I purchased from your hardware store, I found the perfect tree in a jiffy and cut it down in record time." Nathan shot her a conspiratorial look. He knew darn well that she had found the perfect tree, and there was nothing quick about it. But she had to give him credit. He was catching on quickly.

"Thank you, young man." Sal stood a little straighter and stuck out his chest. "You won't find better equipment than mine."

"Or better hot chocolate than at Cindy's Café or better tree-trimming supplies than at Bob's Craft Store. You local business owners have been a huge help in salvaging my Christmas window display. I only hope the rest of the town likes what we've come up with." Nathan donned a convincing worried expression.

The business owners all chimed in at once that he had nothing to worry about, as they dragged him along to introduce to all of their customers. Nancy shot Samantha a dirty look. Sam ignored Nancy and sat back to watch Nathan in awe. The man really was a shark. Once you showed him the way, he went for it, taking no prisoners. She had no doubt most of the town would love him by the end of the bake sale, and the rest would follow once they learned of the little surprise she had planned for tomorrow, which she intended to let him take full credit for. This was the plan. Get everyone in town to love him, to vote for him, and then get the heck out of Redemption in time for Christmas.

Then why did she feel like she'd just gotten burned?

Because she knew in her heart that this wasn't even close to what she really wanted: a night of tender loving care in the arms of a man she had come to adore. Except, adoration on his part had been decidedly absent from the look in his eyes. Tonight, he was all business.

The rest of the evening went by slowly, with Nathan working the crowd and Samantha working the cookie table. Her feet were killing her, and she was more than ready to shed her green velvet dress. She saw very little of him and was dying to continue what they'd started at his place.

Taking a deep breath, she walked over to him and tapped him on the shoulder. He turned around with a smile that looked as though he'd glued it on. A look of relief swept over his features, and he relaxed his lips. "Thank God it's you. I think people are finally starting to come around and see me as something other than a tycoon."

"Imagine if they'd seen you as a tiger like I did this afternoon," she teased. "Ready to show me what you had in mind for my punishment?" She glanced at her watch. "You're officially the boss now."

He hesitated, his shoulders slumping a bit. "It's been a long day. I won't be needing your services tonight, Ms. Darling. As your boss, I am giving you the night off."

She felt her lips part as she stared at him in surprise and then confusion. She bit her bottom lip, trying to figure out what she'd done wrong. His gaze glanced at her lips, and his jaw tightened. Lifting his eyes back to hers, an unreadable mask settled over his features and the tycoon was back.

"Seriously?" was all she could get out.

"I have a headache." He frowned. "I'll see you at the store in the morning." He turned to walk away.

"Try an icepack," she hollered after him. "I've heard it helps." She heard him grumble something about not even an ice bucket would help the state he was in. Obviously being naughty wasn't doing anything more for her than being nice had, and she was beginning to think something was wrong with her.

THURSDAY MORNING DAWNED OMINOUS, the skies looking dangerous, pretty much matching Samantha's mood. There was nothing wrong with her. The more she'd thought about the night before, the angrier she became. She hadn't imagined the flirting and *foreplay* that had gone on while baking cookies in his kitchen. What in the world had happened?

So much for her holiday fling.

Nathan's hot and cold behavior was driving her crazy. He had hinted at wanting her in his bed since she'd first met him, and now when she'd finally decided to give in, he'd changed his mind. The man's arrogance infuriated her. She didn't care how big or powerful he was. He did not get to call all the shots. From this moment on she didn't care if he got down on his knees and begged. She would not sleep with him ever.

Two more days.

If she could make it until Saturday, her sentence would be served and she could go home with her family for Christmas. McScroogy deserved to spend the holiday alone with nothing but a lump of coal.

The bells over the store's door chimed as he walked in to join her, the crow's feet at the corners of his eyes and lines surrounding his mouth more pronounced. He was dressed all in black like the day she'd first met him, his hair no longer loose and free but slicked back and tamed, the air about him screaming authority and control. Yet he looked different. He'd changed somehow. He was still striking and powerful, his presence commanding attention and respect, yet he looked tired. Physically tired and mentally as well, as though being *him* was exhausting. She started to soften but then found her resolve. She could be professional, too.

"Morning, Mr. Snow."

"Come on, Samantha. Call me Nathan."

"Just picking up where we left off, boss." He started to say something, but she held up her hand. "No need to apologize. You were right. We should keep things purely professional."

"I didn't say that."

"I did." She smiled stiffly.

"Whatever. I'm too tired to argue with you, *boss*. It's morning, remember?"

"Didn't sleep well last night?" she asked, hoping he'd tossed relentlessly.

"Not a wink."

"Hmmm, well I *can't* give you the day off. We don't have much time left to fully change your image, and we need every minute. You winning the contest is as much for my benefit as yours."

A flash of sadness and pain crossed his face, but it was so brief Sam wasn't sure if she imagined it or not. "In that much of a hurry to leave, are you?" he asked quietly.

"I've never wanted anything more," she responded defiantly.

"Probably for the best," he muttered, then that damn wall of his slid back into place as he finished loud and clear with, "Okay, then, we'd better get to work."

"My thoughts exactly." She grabbed some non-vintage Santa and Mrs. Claus outfits and headed toward the door. "Follow me," she said over her shoulder.

"What are we doing with those?" he asked.

"Just follow me."

"Great," he grumbled. "This day keeps getting better and better."

They spent all morning going from local business to local business, buying presents for kids of all ages. They took a quick lunch break, and then they bought wrapping supplies and wrapped presents all afternoon. He'd surprised her with his creativity and knowledge about what kids might like. He'd said he was an only child, and Christmases had been nothing but materialistic, yet he put a lot of actual thought into what a child might like. His wrapping job wasn't anywhere near as good as his cooking, but it was the thought that counted. Samantha suspected Nathan was finally getting it.

That evening they pulled into the parking lot of Redemption Elementary School. Nathan's mood had picked up all day with each task they performed, but now he was beaming. "What are we doing here?" he asked.

"Playing Santa. Think you can handle it?" She arched a brow and tried not to smirk. He was making it really hard to stay mad at him when he lit up like a Christmas tree over the idea of helping kids.

"In my sleep." He climbed out of the car with a spring in his step and grabbed the bag of presents from the trunk. "You coming, Mrs. Claus?"

"I wouldn't miss this for the world." She hurried after him, grabbing their costumes along the way. She'd called ahead so the school knew they were coming. They were instructed to sneak in the back door and surprise the kids who were just finishing up and getting ready for their after-school holiday party.

An hour later, Samantha watched Nathan sit patiently with child after child on his knee. She could tell he was struggling not to let his eyes well up with tears. Redemption wasn't a ritzy town. Everyone cared about each other here. Their wishes ranged from simple toys to helping others to the occasional puppy.

It was heartbreaking and endearing and life-changing to watch his reaction.

He managed to say all the right things and touch Samantha in ways she knew she would never get over. Dammit. It wasn't supposed to be like this. She was supposed to endure her punishment as painlessly as possible and then get out. Not fall for the guy. She made up her mind. She might be in for the biggest heartache of her life, but she'd be damned if she'd leave without as many memories as she could gather...starting tonight.

They finished handing out presents and left. He headed straight for the storefront window and set down the empty bag that had held the toys. Then he unbuttoned his Santa jacket and pulled out the fake belly. When he turned around, she was right behind him.

"I should probably go home. I won't be needing—"

"Hmmm, but I will." She placed her hands on his chest which was barely covered with a white undershirt.

"Samantha, what are you doing?"

"Admiring your clothes, Mr. Claus. And who's Samantha? Call me Mrs. C." She slid her hands under his T-shirt and raked her nails up his bare skin.

He sucked in a sharp breath and clenched his jaw. "That's probably not a good idea."

She ran her fingertips down his six-pack, tracing the fine line of hair that disappeared beneath the waistband of his pants. "I think it's the best idea I've had all week."

"Why's that?" he growled.

She boldly reached down and cupped him with her palm. "Because you want me as badly as I want you." She squeezed, and he nearly came undone.

"Sam..."

"Why fight it?" She looked into his eyes. "We know exactly what this is, and what it isn't."

He hesitated. "But your friends said—"

"I knew it!" She stepped back and began pacing. "I knew

there had to be a reason you pulled away from me last night. I can't believe they did that. When I see them, I'm going to—"

He caught her from behind, wrapping his arms around her and pulling her to him tightly. He covered her breast with one hand and slid his other hand down to cup her intimately. This time she was the one to suck in a breath. "It doesn't matter, love," he whispered in her ear. "I'm here now, and you're right. I want you as badly as you do me." He turned her around and cradled her face in his large palms. "Right or wrong, I want you. More importantly...I need you."

And that was all she needed to hear.

She threw her arms around him, and plastered her body to his as she kissed him deeply. He stumbled back a step, and then slid his hands over her behind as he thrust his tongue within her mouth to stroke and mate with hers. After he'd thoroughly robbed her of breath and sent chills soaring through every cell in her body, she whimpered.

He retreated, stroking her face and murmuring words of endearment and encouragement. He slipped his hands beneath her thighs and lifted her high and hard against him. Carrying her to a plush throw rug in the center of the window display, he gently laid her on her back. Shrugging out of his jacket and T-shirt, he whipped off his Santa pants and boxers and stood before her in all his naked glory, giving her a moment to stare unabashedly.

He was a god!

Exquisite male perfection at its best. Tall height, mouth-watering muscles, creamy tanned skin and a gaze that would make the devil himself jealous. He kneeled beside her and slowly pulled off Mrs. C's clothes. Sam had a moment of second thoughts. It was still too light out. Mark had been the first to point out her flaws. Said she was a little too curvy for his tastes. What could she say? She liked to eat. It had never bothered her before, but suddenly she was insecure.

"Wait," she blurted.

"Why?" Nathan asked, his breathing heavier and his gaze heavy-lidded.

"It's too light," she said shyly, not quite meeting his eyes.

"It's not light enough." He tipped her face in his direction so she was forced to look at him. "You're beautiful, Samantha. Let me worship you...*please*."

The please was her undoing. "Okay," she said in barely more than a whisper.

He peeled away the rest of her clothes, and she finally looked at him. What she saw took her breath away. He stared at her as though in awe, his gaze roaming over every ounce of her flesh. Her nipples tightened, her breathing quickened, and her lips parted. His eyes finally met hers.

"I stand corrected. You're not just beautiful, you're an angel, and I am the luckiest man alive." He reached out a hand and stroked her nipple, watching her reaction the whole time.

She arched her back, giving herself to him fully. His smile was so tender and sweet and appreciative. "Nathan, now, please."

"Not yet, sweetheart." He lowered his head and took her nipple in his mouth, sucking hard.

She nearly came undone, crying out his name.

"Easy, baby," he murmured softly, kissing his way down her abdomen. "You're so damn beautiful." He kissed her belly button and then trailed a line of kisses down to her knee and up her inner thigh, finally landing home in the heart of her womanhood.

"Nathan!" she shouted his name and came undone, convulsing in his arms on a wave of pleasure and tears.

He raised above her and slipped inside before her last shutter rippled through her, only to ignite a series of new ones. He thrust harder, holding her hips and pulling her tighter to him as he drove home, murmuring terms of endearment until he stiffened and shouted her name as he came completely undone himself. He collapsed on top of her and rolled to the side, pulling her close to him and cuddling her tenderly. "What have you done to me, woman," he whispered just before he drifted off to sleep.

When his heartbeat slowed and his breathing dipped to that of someone deep asleep, she finally answered with tears in her eyes, "Just loved you, that's all. Even though you're incapable of loving me back."

FRIDAY MORNING NATHAN awoke in his store front window with Samantha gloriously naked and sprawled across his chest. They lay on a thick throw rug in front of the real tree they'd cut down and decorated with traditional, old-fashioned, homemade ornaments. He glanced around and took in the cozy fireplace and vintage Santa and Mrs. Claus. The suits Nathan and Samantha had worn to hand out presents at the orphanage were contemporary knockoffs that served their purpose. He glanced at them and remembered tossing them helter-skelter in his haste to disrobe himself and Ms. Darling who was truly more *darling* than she realized.

They'd come full circle. Surrounded by elves hard at work, but in appropriate clothing and positions this time. He couldn't say the same for himself and Samantha. She was incredible. She'd truly succeeded in taking his mind off the worst time of year for him. She'd done so much more than restore his window display. She brought new life into his store, himself, and the whole damn town. Everyone loved her.

He frowned over the word love.

He never let anyone get that close. He was terrified she wasn't just anyone, and that wasn't part of his plan. Her friends were right. No matter what Samantha said, he knew she wasn't an affair kind of woman. He'd been a fool to give in.

"What's wrong? Why are you frowning?" she asked quietly, startling him.

He looked down at her. "I—I—"

A knock on the window had them both jumping. There was a gap in the curtain, and once again, half the town stood there watching. Only, this time, they were all smiling and giving him the thumbs-up sign instead of staring at him in shock and disapproval.

They really had come full circle, and he didn't have a clue what to do about it.

CHAPTER 7

SAMANTHA DIDN'T GET NATHAN. They'd just experienced an unforgettable, earth-shattering night, and he was acting like they were nothing more than business partners. She'd known what she was setting herself up for, but she secretly hoped she'd had some profound effect on the guy. That maybe he'd discovered the spirit of Christmas and had opened his heart to change...to her.

Instead, he took off, saying he had preparations to make for a surprise Christmas party for his employees. Because he owned so many stores, he usually gave them a Christmas bonus. He stilled planned on doing that, but he'd added a party for this particular store in preparation for the big event the next day.

The window display contest.

What if he didn't win? That meant he could still have her arrested for what she'd done. But if he did win, then she was free to go home on Christmas Eve. Her heart squeezed painfully over the thought of leaving. Funny how what had seemed so important at the start now paled in comparison to the desire to see him look at her in a different way. She knew he wanted her, but she wanted him to love her. Truly love her and put her above himself. He had come so far, but something told her he was incapable of giving her what she needed.

When had her desire to get Mark out of her system turned into a need for Nathan's love?

When he'd held her so tenderly and had looked at her like she was the most precious thing on earth, giving her hope that there could be something more between them. Maybe tonight she would tell him how she felt.

She spent the rest of the day finishing the final touches on the storefront window, while Nathan made the arrangements for the party. He'd poked his head in for brief seconds here and there, but mostly avoided her all day. Refusing to let it get her down, Samantha donned a silk baby blue metallic cocktail dress in the same shade as her eyes and three inch silver heels. She stood by the door when a limo pulled up alongside the curb. Donning the sexiest smile she could, she slipped inside and frowned.

The driver said, "Mr. Snow will meet you at the restaurant, ma'am. There's champagne and hors d'oeuvres if you'd care for any. He closed the door and climbed into the front and then drove away.

She was being bought off. Nathan had given her a limo ride with fine champagne and caviar, yet he hadn't given her himself. It cheapened what they'd shared. She only had one more night with him, and she had her work cut out for her.

She slid out of the limo, took a deep breath, and marched inside on a mission. The first person she ran into was Roz. Samantha stiffened, expecting the pit-bull to unleash her wrath. Instead, the petite silver-haired dynamo studied

Samantha until she squirmed and the woman smiled ever so slightly. She was in control, and they both knew it. Yet she didn't rip her apart. Maybe she was in a holiday mood. Whatever the reason, Sam was grateful.

"Happy holidays," Samantha said.

"Same to you," Roz responded, looking pained to add, "You did a great job on the storefront window."

"Thank you. Na—Mr. Snow was a huge part in putting it all together."

The pit-bull was back, on edge, and ready to bear its fangs if Sam said the wrong thing. "You've changed him. He's not the same man he was before you got here."

"Oh, well, I'm sorry. I didn't mean to—"

"Thank you."

"Excuse me?"

"You have no idea what that poor boy's been through." For a moment her features softened into a look of maternal love, but just as quickly she snarled, "Hurt him, and it'll be the last thing you do." Then she marched away.

Nathan was the one who had avoided Samantha all day, *not* the other way around. Quite frankly, she'd had enough.

It was time she and McScroogy had a talk.

NATHAN FINISHED HANDING out the last of the Christmas bonuses to his staff. They had more than earned it. Their help had touched him deeply, which disturbed him immensely. He'd never cared before. In truth, he'd cared too much, and that terrified him, so he'd never admit it, even to himself. He'd gotten away with pretending he didn't care because he knew first-hand what it was like to care and then get hurt.

Damn Samantha Darling.

She'd changed him, and he was afraid he would never be able to change back. He didn't want to find the spirit of Christmas. It held too many painful memories. He didn't want to make friends. He didn't want to care what people thought of him. He didn't want to lose his ruthless businessman image. He didn't want to fall in love....

But, dammit, that's exactly what had happened.

He knew what he had to do. No matter how much it hurt, he knew it was the right thing. Give her a gift that wasn't materialistic and came straight from his heart. Give her what he knew she wanted more than anything else.

Set her free and let her go home to be with her family.

He didn't need to drag her down with him into his lonely depressing world, especially during this time of year. She was light and beautiful and kind and fun. He was the total opposite. She deserved happiness with no brooding or darkness. He couldn't promise any of that. So, he would do what he always did: put up his wall and shut her out. Better to hurt her now than before she fell in love with him, too.

Nathan felt a tap on his shoulder. He turned around and inhaled sharply. Samantha stood before him looking much more stunning than any angel on the top of a Christmas tree. She looked a little wary and nervous, and it killed him to know he was responsible. Her stubborn determination kicked in and she stood a little straighter, causing his heart to swell with love and pride.

He frowned and cleared his throat, smoothing his black tuxedo, and then running a hand over slicked-back hair. His armor. "Ms. Darling, you look lovely this evening. I hope everything is to your liking."

"No, actually, it isn't. I have an issue I'd like to discuss," she said firmly.

"I thought you might." He pulled out a legal document from the inside of his jacket. "Happy holidays." He handed the paper to her.

"What's this?"

"Your gift," he said, keeping his face blank.

Her delicate eyebrows drew together as she opened the paper. "You're giving me my freedom?"

"Precisely. From this moment forward I am releasing you from your punishment, and I will not press charges now or in the future over this matter. In other words, Ms. Darling, you are free to go."

"But...what about the window display contest?"

"Win or lose, it doesn't matter. Your debt has been paid."

She looked as though he'd slapped her in the face. "Oh my God, I'm such an idiot."

Now he was the one to frown. "I'm not sure I follow you."

She clenched her jaw and glared at him. "Oh, I'm sure you follow me exactly. Cold and ruthless doesn't begin to describe you. You never cared about winning that contest. You simply refused to release me from my punishment until I gave you what you wanted. You're worse than Scrooge. You're a coward. And to think I let myself fall in love with you." She whirled around and fled, leaving Nathan stunned and reeling, with a room full of guests who'd overheard every word.

He glanced at the crowd and watched face after face turn into frowns of disapproval and glares of anger. He couldn't blame them. He was mad as hell at himself. He'd only tried to give her what he thought she wanted. He had no idea she loved him, too. He still didn't think he was good enough for her. What if he brought her down with him? What if he ruined her life? What if he made her sad? What if he changed her, too? He'd never forgive himself.

He was scared to death and, for once in life, let everything he was feeling show raw and real across his face.

"What the hell is wrong with all of you?" Roz barked. "Can't you see he loves her, too? In his foolish, misguided way, he's trying to save her from himself because he doesn't think he's worthy. He has no idea how much he's changed. He does deserve to be happy, no matter how much the opposite has been drilled into him."

Could Roz be right? Did he and Samantha actually stand a chance? This time when he looked up, half the room was teary-eyed right along with Roz and himself.

"What are ya waiting for, Mr. Snow?" Betty said, sniffling.

"It's plain as day you two belong together," Sal added.

"Go after that girl," Bob chimed in.

"It's all so romantic," Cindy said on a dreamy sigh.

"They're right," Nancy, his longtime rival, said quietly. "You have changed. It's awful to love someone and not have them love you back," she let her longing for him show on her face as she looked him in the eye, "but to have someone love you back and not tell you would be a downright shame. Forget the contest. I forfeit, and you win, so don't be stupid. Be happy, Nathan. And who knows. Maybe we'll find a way to work together someday." She smiled her first ever genuine smile toward him.

Roz stepped forward and hugged him hard in a rare display of affection, then she pulled back and donned her most stern expression. "Well? What the hell are you going to do about it?"

His smile came slow and sweet as he responded with a twinkle in his eye, "I think it's time I gave a Christmas present to myself. Take the next two days off, folks. For the first time ever Snow's Antiques will be closed for the holidays. Merry Christmas to all and to all a good night." He winked as the room broke out into wild and rowdy cheers, and he ran to his car.

IT WAS SATURDAY MORNING. Christmas Eve. Samantha's favorite time of the year. But the last thing she felt like doing was celebrating. Last year when her fiancé had cheated on her, it had been heartbreaking. Yet it didn't compare to finding out the man she loved didn't love her back. That was devastating. It was her own fault. He'd made it clear he wanted no strings attached. She knew he had commitment issues, yet she'd let herself fall anyway.

How could he possibly have looked at her and held her and made love to her that way if he didn't love her? She was usually good at reading people, and his actions had said so much more than his words ever could. She'd known he had a hard time expressing himself, but she'd been so sure.

She was a fool.

How could he have sent her away so easily? The second after he'd gotten what he wanted, he'd turned right back into his old self. And it hurt like hell. She'd driven to her parents, poured her heart out to her mother, and then went to bed early and cried herself to sleep. Now today her parents had been acting strangely all day.

When she'd finally cornered them, they told her she'd

ruined the surprise. They had invited Amber and Ellen to their annual Christmas Eve party. Her sister's family and brother's families would be there like always. Sam had complained that she was in no mood for a party, but they insisted she not break tradition. This was exactly what she needed.

It was their house. What could she say? She'd gone along with it because she had no other choice, even though the spirit of Christmas was nowhere to be found this year. The doorbell rang. Her brother and sister and their families were already there.

"Samantha, can you get that?" her mother asked from the kitchen.

"Sure thing, Mom." Sam went to the door, plastered on a fake smile, and opened it.

"Hey, babe, what's shakin'?" Elfish Ellen asked, giving her a quick hug and barging right in.

Amazon Amber rolled her eyes and then looked at Sam and chuckled. "She's a character."

"To say the least," Sam said, but couldn't quite bring herself to laugh.

Amber hugged her and stepped inside as well. "How are you?"

"I take it Mom told you," Sam said, not surprised.

"No...he did," Amber said quietly, surprising Sam.

"*He* did?"

She nodded. "He never wanted to hurt you, you know."

"Speaking of that. I have a bone to pick with both you and Ellen. If you hadn't made that phone call, he wouldn't have pulled away and then been so freaked out when we finally did sleep together." Sam held up her hands. "You know what? It doesn't matter. He ended up hurting me anyway."

Ellen joined them with a glass of spiked punch. "He's hurting too, hon."

Sam scowled. "Yeah, hurting all the way to the bank. He got exactly what he wanted: sex with me, a new image, and a winning window display."

"Ever think maybe he set you free because he thought he was giving you what you wanted? Your freedom and Christmas with your family?" Ellen asked gently.

"No, yes, I don't know," Sam said miserably, tearing up all over again. "I'm so confused. I could have sworn he loved me, too." She was outright sobbing now. "You should have seen how much he changed. He has more Christmas spirit than I do, yet he won't admit it. He loves those kids at the orphanage, he loves the town of Redemption, and I thought he loved me. I guess I was wrong."

"You know what you need?" Amber asked.

"What?" Sam snuffled.

"An early Christmas present." Amber hugged her hard. "Now wipe your nose. The Santa your mom always hires will be here soon."

"Great." Sam blew her nose. "Do I look awful?"

"No," Amber scoffed.

"Liar." Sam attempted a smile. "I'd better get that star on top of the tree I guess."

"Come on. We'll help." Ellen led the way into the living room where Samantha's brother, sister, their families and her parents were waiting.

"Here you go, sweetie." Sam's mother handed her the star and tried not to get teary-eyed.

"We're so happy to have you home in time to do this, pumpkin." Her father wrapped her in a bear hug, not even attempting to hide his tears.

Sam almost started crying all over again. She took the star and climbed the ladder her father held next to their seven-foot-high Christmas tree while her family looked on in anticipation. Reaching and placing the star in the perfect spot, she smiled a genuine smile for the first time since leaving Redemption.

Just as her brother plugged in the tree and the star twinkled on top, the doorbell rang. Her sister went to answer the door while her nieces and nephews squealed in delight and then shouted, "Santa's here, Santa's here!"

Sam's parents did this every year. It had become a tradition that no one outgrew. A second later, jolly ole Saint Nick rounded the corner with a bag full of presents. He sat in a big chair that Sam's father had placed right beside the Christmas tree.

"Ho, ho, ho," said Santa, in his big booming Santa voice. "Who wants to sit on my lap?"

The children quickly lined up in front of him without a single fuss about the order they wound up in. They all knew that Santa had a way of finding out who was naughty or nice, and being naughty meant all you got was a lump of coal. Needless to say, they were all on their best behavior.

One by one they told Santa what they most desired for Christmas this year. When they were done, Santa told them all that they'd been very good boys and girls, and then he reached into his bag and gave them each a present. Finally, he turned to the adults. He didn't make them sit on his lap. He stood and went to each of them, one by one, and asked what they wanted most. It was the same every year, no matter how old they grew, they still had to face judgment day in front of Santa and tell him if they'd been good or not. And then he would give them a present as well. Sam's parents had always pre-selected the presents and paid the Santa to hand those out as well.

This Santa was good. He had the scoop on everyone and knew just how far to go in teasing each of them, and then finally giving them their gift. The children loved the thought that their parents, aunts, uncles and grandparents weren't always perfect, either.

Finally, it was Samantha's turn. Her friends had been right. This was exactly what she needed, and she found herself smiling and enjoying her favorite holiday despite the heartache.

"So tell me, Ms. Darling, have you been naughty or nice this year?" Santa asked as he stood in front of her, his enormous belly bouncing as he talked.

"A little of both, I guess," she said honestly, suspecting her parents had given him an earful.

"I see. And are you sorry for what you've done?"

"I'm sorry for breaking the law, but I'm not sorry for what resulted because of it. As painful as it might be, I will never forget my time in Redemption." She stared off thoughtfully. "The people, the store, my boss...all of it."

"Given the chance, would you do it all over again?"

"In a heartbeat," she answered immediately, and then blinked, realizing it was true.

It didn't matter that she fell in love with a man who could never love her back. He'd given her as much as he could. She would never regret her time with him. She'd done what she'd set out to do: teach Nathan Snow what the spirit of Christmas was all about. And she now understood he had given her what he thought she wanted. Her freedom. He hadn't tried to give her something monetary. He truly "got" it. If he couldn't give her himself, then this was the next best thing.

"You would do it over knowing how it would all end?" Santa asked in a skeptical tone. "Why?"

"He was worth it," she answered simply.

Santa smiled and then surprised her and everyone else in the room when he threw her over his shoulder and headed for the door.

"Wh-what are you doing?" she sputtered.

"Giving you your present," he said without stopping, then added for the kids benefit, "Ms. Darling needs a good talking to before I decide whether or not to give her a lump of coal."

They stepped outside, and he set her on her feet, closing the door on the gasps and giggles coming from children and adults alike.

"What the hell do you think you're doing?" she asked. Santa or no Santa, this guy had a lot of nerve carrying his job this far.

"Giving you your present," he said.

"Let me guess...a lump of coal," she said, scowling at him.

"No, this," he answered, seconds before swooping down and covering her mouth with his own. Before she could utter a single protest, he wrapped his arms around her and pulled her in close...or as close as his big belly would allow.

As soon as his lips touched hers, she knew.

She pulled away briefly to whisper, "Nathan?"

"I love you," was all he said, as he stared into her eyes with all his heart.

She let out a cry and threw her arms around him, pressing her lips to his.

He broke away to say in a low growl, "Baby, I need you closer."

She yanked off his hat and pulled his beard over his head as he unbuttoned his coat and tossed it aside with his fake belly. He had barely stepped out of his Santa pants when she launched herself at him, wrapping her legs around his waist. He caught her beneath her thighs and pressed her up against the door. She plunged her hands into his hair and her eyes nearly crossed as he slipped his tongue between her lips to mate with her own.

"Say it again," she said on a soft sob, tears streaming down her face as she wiped away his.

"I love you, Samantha Darling. With all my soul, for better or worse—which I can't promise there won't be a lot of worse —until death do us part. Please say you'll marry me. I can't live without you, baby."

She gasped. "Yes! I love you so much it hurts, and there is no worse with you. None of us is perfect. You're flawed and ornery and mine, McScroogy. And nothing but death will ever make us part if I have my way."

"I *am* Santa, and it *is* Christmas Eve. The time when magical things happen. You loving me is proof of that. I have pull, and I say you can have your way in anything you want."

"Good. I say I want you for Christmas, Santa baby."

"Done." He pressed a quick kiss to her lips and set her down. "We'd better get in there before the kids start to wonder."

"Wait." She grabbed his Santa Suit and hid it in the garage then took his hand and led the way inside.

"Aunt Sam, what happened. Are you in trouble? Did Santa give you coal?"

"I'd say Santa's very happy with me. Look what he brought me?" She pulled Nathan into the room after her, and she met her mother's eyes. "A fiancé."

Jaws dropped, and everyone started to cheer. There were lots of hugs and well wishes, and then Amber said, "Got any brothers?"

Nathan chuckled and responded, "No, but I have lots of friends in very powerful places." He winked.

"Careful, ladies. Being naughty can get you into a lot of trouble," Sam said, staring up at Nathan and adoring every ounce of her trouble with a capital T.

"Being nice can be oh so boring," Amber chimed in on a grunt. "Personally, I've had my fill of boring."

"Cheers to that," Ellen said and raised her glass of eggnog. "To being naughty and loving every minute of it."

Oh, Nathan, Samantha thought, *You have no idea what you just started....*

JINGLE ALL THE WAY

CHAPTER 1

"CHRISTMAS EVE IS such a magical day, don't you think?" Amber Evans asked with stars in her whiskey-colored eyes that glowed with love. She watched her jolly blond giant fiancé, Kip Covington, head to the bar to bring back champagne to toast their engagement. Tossing her long dark hair over her shoulder with a dreamy sigh, she looked blissfully happy.

Magical? Not so much, Ellen Patterson thought with a pout as she stared at her best friend with what she feared was happiness-envy.

Amber was Amazon tall and had been a volleyball MVP in college, while Kip was a retired NBA all-star with godlike looks. He could seriously be Thor's twin. They were both competitive and stubborn and always followed the rules, playing fair. Thank God he'd thrown the book out the window and took a chance that she might do the same. They were perfect for each other. If she'd lost him, neither of them would have recovered. Now she stood among them as an engaged woman to a man who truly did love her.

Amazon Amber plus a reformed Scrooge McDunky equaled a perfect match.

"I couldn't agree more," said the blue-eyed, blonde Barbie doll, Mrs. Samantha Snow. She stared after her brand-new husband with his devilish dark looks, the reformed Nathan McScroogy, who stood beside Kip at the bar of their wedding reception. "Christmas Eve is special. 'Tis the season of giving selflessly, and I intend to give my husband plenty of gifts starting tonight."

"Easy for you two to say," Ellen grumbled. "I know I'm whining, but I really thought I would meet someone tonight of all nights." She held up her hands to ward off what she knew was coming. "Don't even go there, you two. Scrooge McBoring doesn't count, and no amount of work will reform that boy."

Nathan's friend, Jason Moore—of Moore and Griswold Attorneys at Law—was more boring than any single female should have to put up with. Of course, she'd gotten stuck walking down the aisle with him. Amber was the lucky one who scored big with Kip, although his seven-foot frame never would have worked with Ellen's petite five-foot body. Still, at least he was fun. Getting snowed in for days with Jason at Kip's romantic ski lodge had been pure torture. Now that they were rescued and the reception was in full swing, she'd seriously had high hopes.

"I don't think he's that bad. Maybe you just need to give him a chance," Amber said with pity in her eyes.

"Um, that would be a negative," Ellen countered. "Even I have my limits."

"Well, I'm sure you'll find someone else to call your own very soon," Amber added encouragingly.

"Ha! Not likely," Ellen sputtered, running a hand through her fiery red hair, probably ruining the sophisticated style Samantha had worked so hard to create, but Ellen couldn't help it. She was terrified her best friends were going to move on without her, and then what would her life be like?

When Ellen got antsy, she tended to get into trouble.

The three of them had been friends forever and worked together at the same advertising firm in Boston, which Ellen was grateful for. They'd each bailed her out more times than she could count. She hated to admit it, but she was afraid to be alone. As one of six children, she came from a big family and didn't know how to exist by herself. She'd never had to because she'd met Amber and Samantha in college and stayed close through work. But now all of that was about to change. They were going to leave her, and she didn't know how to cope.

"I thought when we got here I would finally have some fun," she said, as she shoved her depressing thoughts aside and did what she always did: stirred the pot. "There seemed like so much potential with all the single men here, but they're stiffs. Not one of them wanted to kiss me under the mistletoe."

"Imagine that," Amber said dryly. "If I'm not mistaken, you don't even know many of them."

"We're young, we're single, we're hot...what more do we need to know?"

"Maybe you need to tone it down a bit," Sam added gently. "You have so much to offer, but most men can't handle your, um, energy."

"Then they're not real men, are they?" Ellen said in frustration. "If only I could find a *real* man, maybe then I would finally have some fun." Maybe then she could put her fears aside and stop worrying about what the future would be like as the last musketeer, the last amigo, the last everything.

Kip and Nate walked back to the women, carrying drinks for a toast. At least she would always have the Captain and Jack. They could be her new threesome.

"Where's Jason?" Nate asked.

If you asked Ellen, Jason hadn't been the best choice as a groomsman for Nathan. But poor Nate didn't have any family and no other associates he really trusted, so Jason had been his last resort.

Doing what he does best, making himself scarce, Ellen thought, but said, "No idea." Now, there was a wimp of a man if ever she saw one.

The door to the reception hall burst open, and a guy around six-feet-tall stepped inside. He had dark eyes and a dark buzz cut, wearing jeans and a black leather jacket. He slipped off his coat and slung it over his shoulder, revealing a heavily muscled frame with tattoos on his arm. His five o'clock shadow was actually the length of a short beard, and a small scar marred his forehead just above his thick black eyebrow. He looked tough and serious and a little angry as he scanned the crowded room. His whole aura screamed wounded soul; hell bent on revenge. There was something so familiar about him, but she couldn't quite put her finger on it.

As maid of honor, Ellen knew Amber wasn't about to let anyone ruin her best friend's day. Amber's radiant smile transformed into a firm line as she narrowed her eyes at the uninvited guest and stepped forward, ready to run interference. Kip grabbed her arm and shook his head, and she reluctantly backed down. He studied the man as though he sensed something familiar as well.

Ellen shrugged. Familiar or not, he sure seemed interesting. "Now there's a man who looks like he knows how to have fun," she said, unable to help herself. "Time to get this party started."

McMuscles appeared to be the exact kind of challenge Ellen needed right now to take her mind off her worries.

"Ellen, I don't think…" Amber's voice trailed off as the room grew quiet as a morgue.

The man searched the crowd until he found Nathan's father, then his eyes filled with satisfaction as he said in a deep gruff voice, "I've waited a lifetime to do this. Alexander Snow, you're under arrest."

Nathan stepped forward. "Who the hell are you?"

The man's intense gaze met Nathan's and hardened as he said bitterly, "I'm Detective MacKenzie Johnson … your long-lost brother. Merry Christmas."

MAC SCANNED the crowd that had erupted into frenzied shouts and accusations after he'd dropped the bomb. He'd waited so long for a little payback … a little justice. Alexander Snow was his father. His biological father, anyway. Mac and Nathan both looked exactly like their father, rather than their mothers, but that was as far as the connection went. Alexander had never laid claim to Mac, or so much as acknowledged he even existed. Mac's poor mother had been a young college intern in Snow's business when he'd cheated on his wife and knocked her up just one month before he'd gotten his wife pregnant with Nathan. Once he found out his wife was pregnant, he fired Mac's mother and never looked back.

"What the hell do you think you're doing?" Alexander Snow sputtered, looking pale and distraught as Mac cuffed him in front of his scandalized wife and all their friends.

"Locking you up and cutting off the outside world," Mac growled, nailing him with as much venom and hatred as he could muster, "same as you did to me at the tender age of ten." Alexander paled even more, which Mac hadn't thought possible, and his wife looked ready to swoon.

Mac was Snow's firstborn, his rightful heir, yet he'd grown up in an orphanage while Nathan had everything handed to him on a silver platter, none the wiser. When Mac's mother died unexpectedly in a car crash when he was ten, he'd had no one else to claim him. He'd tried to say Snow was his father, but Alexander denied the claim and turned his back on him, knowing he was too old for anyone else to adopt him. A year later, Snow started donating money to the orphanage, probably out of guilt. The same orphanage his "real" son Nathan now donated to, but it was too late. Mac had grown up alone, without anyone. Needless to say he didn't trust easily. He hated his father—hated them both—for all they stood for, vowing one day to make them pay.

That day was today.

"You can't do this." Nathan stepped forward. "It's my wedding day."

Mac had spent his life relying on no one, working hard, putting himself through college, and earning the respect of his colleagues in the Boston Police Department. They were all the family he would ever need, and even with them, he never truly let anyone in. Because when you let someone in and gave yourself hope, you got burned.

"I can and I did, so get over it." Mac stared his brother—who looked so much like him it was uncanny—down and shrugged as though he didn't give a damn, even though the child within him still did. "I'd say I'm sorry, but I'm not."

"Why are you arresting him?" His brother's lovely blonde wife asked in a sweet voice.

Mac felt a twinge of regret at the sadness he'd obviously caused her.

Nathan placed a protective arm around her bare shoulders, drawing her close as if shielding her from Mac. "It's all right, darling, I'll get to the bottom of this," Nathan stated with a black glare which would make a normal man cringe. Only Mac wasn't normal, he was blood, and more like him than he cared to admit. "Do not remove my father until you tell me the charges."

"You may not want to claim him once you know the true Alexander Snow. The lying, cold-blooded, uncaring bastard he really is." Mac was finding it hard to remain in control as people whispered around him.

"I asked what you're charging him with." Nathan's voice sounded as lethal as Mac's, and his brother moved so his body was now in front of his wife's.

"Importing illegal drugs through his company."

The crowd gasped, and Nathan frowned. "No way. The old man might do a lot of things I don't approve of, but drugs? I'm not buying it, and I'm guessing you can't prove it."

"Like hell I can't, and I don't answer to you." Mac glared at him. "Trust me, *brother*, I wouldn't be here if I didn't have proof." He leaned forward just as menacingly. "By the way, you can stop being a hypocrite and writing checks to the orphanage...my *home*." Then he pulled on Alexander and started dragging him to the door. "They have me," Mac called over his shoulder and finished with, "and that's all they need." Then he walked outside, shoved his father in the back of his unmarked squad car, and drove away.

"WHAT THE HELL WAS THAT?" Nathan asked, looking ashen and visibly shaken.

"I don't know, but I'm going to find out," Ellen said. She was on a mission, and once she set her mind to something, there was no stopping her, regardless of the consequences. She was a sucker for taking in lost strays and trying to heal them. McMuscles needed healing for sure, but that wasn't the mission she was on. No one hurt her friends. The man looked dangerous. Like the kind who could inflict a whole lot of hurt without an ounce of remorse. She wouldn't put it past him to fight dirty to get what he wanted. He just had no idea she was the queen of dirty.

"No!" Sam chimed in, an alarmed look on her face as she grabbed Ellen's arm.

"Uh, yeah, no. I'm with Sam here, Ellen," Amber chimed in. "You're not exactly the most 'judicial' one of our group."

"But I *am* the most free at the moment," Ellen said. "You and Nate—no matter what you say—are about to go on your honeymoon. And you *are* going! You have worked too long and hard for this, and you owe it to Sam, Nate. Besides, your father has a whole team of attorneys and more than enough money to bail himself out."

Nathan and Samantha just blinked at her.

"Amber, you and Kip just got engaged," Ellen continued.

"You two need to start massive wedding planning if you're going to succeed in getting married on Christmas Eve next year as well. You of all people should know how long it takes to book places for a wedding and reception."

Kip and Amber looked thoughtful, as though considering her words.

"Look, guys," Ellen hammered her point home. "I am the only one who is single and frankly doesn't have a whole lot to do these days. I need this. Please trust me and let me take care of this little *problem*."

"I don't know, El," Sam said. "It's a lot of responsibility to take on. Nathan's father's freedom is on the line."

"I know. But we all know he's a big boy and more than capable of taking care of himself. I will be sure to follow up with him as well as his attorneys in Nathan's place to make sure everything goes smoothly. You can count on me. I'm up for it."

"I have to say I'm with Sam on this," Amber added. "It's a lot of responsibility."

"Which I am more than capable of handling," Ellen stated firmly. "For crying out loud I handle million dollar campaigns on a daily basis. I know I sometimes bend the rules a bit and get into trouble, but you girls are always the ones to bail me out and take care of everything. I think it's time I proved myself."

They still looked doubtful.

Ellen looked them each in the eye and tried honesty. "I need to be the one in charge, saving the day. I need to know you trust me to be an adult. I am a smart, savvy, advertising executive. I think I can handle one disgruntled, unexpected, secret half-brother and his plans to ruin your life." She sent

Nathan and Kip a pleading look, knowing her chances of winning the men over were much more favorable than winning over her best friends.

"Okay," Nathan said. "On one condition." He gave Ellen a no-nonsense look. "You let Jason help."

Ellen opened her mouth to object but thought better of it. It wouldn't be too hard to lose McBoring. "Deal," she said.

Sam blinked, looking shocked. "Nate, sweetheart, are you sure? We don't have to do this."

"Yes we do, my love," he said, taking her hands. "I don't know who this MacKenzie Johnson really is, but if what he says is true, then it doesn't surprise me. My father is a piece of work. If he truly left my brother—who is basically my twin— to fend for himself since the age of ten, then so help me God if I stick around, I'll kill the old man myself. I might have grown up privileged, but you and I both know I might as well have grown up in the orphanage I so love. And to think I had a brother my age there all along is just unfathomable. And the obvious fact that he hates me breaks my heart."

"All right then, darling, honeymoon it is," Sam said with love and understanding and fierce protectiveness shining bright within her eyes as she cupped his face and kissed him tenderly.

"I can still help if you need it, El," Amber said.

"While I appreciate that, Amber, I've seen you and Kip in action," Ellen said. "I know you guys are in love, but trust me, it's going to take a miracle for you both to work out the wedding plans in one year's time without killing each other."

"She does have a point," Kip interjected, earning Amber's scowl. "Awww, come on, baby," he said softly, drawing her into his arms. "Half the fun is sparring with you, but we really do need to get moving if we're going to set the date for next Christmas Eve. I know exactly how we should plan the wedding. Do you know how soon places book?"

"I have a few plans of my own. Do *you* know who you're talking to?" Amber snapped, stubbornly refusing to cave.

"Oh, just the love of my life," he responded softly, tilting her face up to his.

Her whole body softened, and she melted into him. "Okay, babe," she said with a dreamy sigh, laying a big one on him, and just like that it was settled.

Ellen tried not to roll her eyes. "I promise I won't let you all down," she said with determination. "I *will* get to the bottom of this if it's the last thing I do."

MacKenzie Johnson had no idea who *he* was about to deal with.

CHAPTER 2

"WHAT THE HELL do you mean, Snow's a free man?" Mac asked his captain the next afternoon in his office at the BPD precinct. It was Christmas day. He always worked because spending the holiday alone was too depressing. His captain had joined him ever since his wife died. Mac shut the door behind him, tuning out the sounds of voices and phones and people milling about.

Captain Scott sighed, rubbing his bald head. The man had been formidable in his day, but years of running a busy precinct had taken a toll on him. He looked tired, and suddenly much older than his middle-aged years. "Don't start with me, Detective Johnson," he finally said. "You and I both know you've been after the Snows since you joined the force. Hell, probably long before that."

"Yes, but I had just cause to finally lock up the old man. That shipment of cocaine was on his boat. And now you're telling me he's out? Just like that?" Mac paced back and forth, anger and frustration gnawing at his insides. Where the hell was the justice in that?

"Sit down before you make me dizzy, son." His captain waited until he complied. "Snow claims the employees involved forged his signature, signing off on that shipment. That he knew nothing about it and is willing to take a polygraph test to prove it."

"Don't tell me you buy that load of crap?" Mac surged to his feet.

"I said sit down," his captain growled in a voice he rarely had to use on Mac, which prompted Mac to slowly lower himself into his chair and strive for a calm he didn't feel. "What I'm telling you is that the matter is being looked into," his captain finally responded.

Mac clenched his jaw before asking in a neutral voice, "What does that mean exactly?"

His captain hesitated. "That he's out on bail for now."

"I see." Mac scrubbed his buzz cut with his hand. "Must be nice to have money."

"Money, and a firecracker of an elf on your side." His captain's lips twisted into an amused grin.

Mac narrowed his eyes. "Elf you say?"

"Yeah, I've never seen anything like it." Captain Scott chuckled. "This little bitty thing with fiery red hair and sparkling green eyes came charging in here this morning, and I swore I heard bells jingling. She couldn't have been more than five feet tall, but that didn't mean a blessed thing. I pity the man who tries to tame her. She stormed all over this place in a no-nonsense fashion until she got what she wanted."

Mac clenched his fists. "And that was?"

"Alexander Snow on a silver platter. She posted his bail, and there wasn't a damn thing we could do."

Mac cursed under his breath. He vaguely remembered

someone of that description at Nathan Snow's wedding reception. He remembered thinking she was attractive in a unique and interesting sort of way, but then he had pushed all thoughts other than taking Alexander Snow down out of his mind. Now he realized he should have paid more attention. Who was she?

More importantly, what exactly was she up to?

"Go. You're not any use to me until you work out whatever this all is," Captain Scott said, but then nailed Mac with a hard look. "Deal with it, Johnson. I want this finished once and for all."

"Oh, I'll deal with it, Captain," Mac said with a low grumble. "Count on it."

"ELLEN, there's someone here to see you," Tina Warsaw said as she poked her head inside Ellen's office, her shoulder-length, sandy blonde bob brushing her slender shoulders.

Tina was a nice person but all business, with no time for a personal life. A young, energetic workaholic who wanted nothing more than to climb the proverbial ladder of success at Creative Creations just as fast as she could. That's why she worked every Christmas. Ellen usually took Christmas off and spent it with her family, but this year she couldn't handle listening to her mother lament that she was the only one of her babies who wasn't married yet.

"Thanks, Tina," Ellen responded. "Send him right in."

Tina's brow wrinkled in confusion. "How did you know it was a man?"

Ellen's lips tipped up into a small smile of satisfaction.

McMuscles wasn't the only one who had a few tricks up his sleeve. "Let's just say I was expecting him."

Detective Johnson strode into her office in his snug jeans, tight T-shirt, and leather jacket, looking more like a hitman than a cop. God, he was hot. He had bad boy written over every delicious inch of him. Ellen loved bad boys, but this one threatened the happiness of her best friends. If Nathan was unhappy, then Samantha surely would be. Ellen wouldn't let that happen, no matter how much MacKenzie's wounded soul called to her.

"What do you want?" he asked, his voice low and gruff, striking a chord deep within her. He stared at her with such dark, intense eyes, she swallowed hard. He had intimidation down to a science with his chiseled jawline and the scar above his eyes, but Ellen had never been one to back down easily.

"What do you mean?" she asked nonchalantly, blinking up at him with the wide-eyed innocent look she'd perfected, hoping like hell he couldn't tell how turned on she was by his mere presence.

"You might have been in the wedding, but you're not related to Snow. I did my homework. This has nothing to do with you, so I repeat, what do you want?"

"This has everything to do with me," she said, dropping the act and adding a certain amount of growl to her own voice. She surged to her feet and stepped around her desk, getting right in his face.

His full lips parted as though he were taken aback, but then he stood his ground, staring down at her, hands fisted at his sides. "Why?" he ground out through clenched teeth.

"Because you're messing with my friends!" She poked him

hard in the chest when what she really wanted to do was punch him.

He moved faster than she'd ever seen anyone move and caught her hand in his much larger one. "So?"

Ignoring the way he made her pulse pick up, she pulled her hand out of his before he could tell the effect he had on her and replied, "*So* friends are family, and I don't take family lightly."

He grunted. "Well, I don't take family at all."

"Apparently." She snorted, crossing her arms and shaking her head in pity. "You obviously have issues." She sighed in regret. "As much as I'd like to help you with them, you've created a conflict of interest for me." She let her gaze wander the length of him appreciatively and then shrugged. "Your loss." Looking him square in the eye, she finished with, "Make no mistake, Scrooge MacGruff...you hurt them, I hurt you back."

He arched a brow as though a war between interest and frustration battled inside him. She had that effect on most people. She fascinated them, but they had no idea what to do with her. Shrugging off his daze, he responded with an authoritative tone, "The law's the law, sweetheart. Break it, you're gonna pay. That's exactly what Snow did."

"Says you. His attorneys say otherwise."

He narrowed his eyes. "Prove it."

She smiled like the Cheshire cat. "We intend to."

"Again with the *we.*" He made a set of air quotes. "Stay out of my way, and we'll get along just fine. Do I make myself clear?"

"Oh, it's clear that you hate your father," she said with a knowing tone. "I can't blame you for that. Mr. Snow doesn't exactly give off the warm and fuzzies, but Nathan is nothing like him. Okay, so maybe he used to be like him, but that was only because he was bitter after having a hard life growing up."

Mac let out a harsh laugh.

"Believe it or not, Nate probably grew up even more alone than you did. You had a loving mother until you were ten, and then you had the other kids in the orphanage. Nate didn't have any brothers or sisters, and his parents bought him presents as companions because they were never around. Even his nanny wasn't very friendly."

"I'm sure living in a mansion surrounded by expensive toys was rough," Mac said sarcastically.

"You might have had it rougher, but I'd bet Nate was lonelier."

"Whatever. That's not my problem," Mac said with a devil-may-care attitude, but Ellen saw the shadows lying just beneath the surface.

She wanted to pounce and take advantage of his vulnerability, but she didn't. Dammit, she was a softy. Her tone gentled against her will and she relented a hair, adding, "It's not too late to get to know your brother. I know Nate wants to get to know you."

Mac looked startled for a minute, probably over having revealed anything, and then his face hardened. "I have no interest in having any kind of relationship with Nathan Snow. I don't do relationships, period. I'm simply doing my job in putting his father behind bars. Or at least I was until you intervened."

"Oh, I can't take all the credit for that. I just had a role in saving you from yourself." She patted him on the chest. "You'll thank me one day, MacGruff. Wait and see."

"Fraternizing with the enemy," Jason Moore of Moore and Griswold Attorneys at Law said from the doorway of Ellen's office. "Typical Ellen."

He was a handsome enough man, impeccably dressed with light brown eyes and hair perfectly styled, yet ninety percent of the time his face was buried in his smartphone. She'd dubbed him McBoring and had moved on. End of story. Except once again Nathan had paired them together. If it wasn't for Sam, Ellen might have had a mind to side with Mac and sink Jason's battleship, but she couldn't do that. She had to prove to her friends that she had their backs this time, even if it meant playing nice in the sandbox with a bottom feeder.

"Jason Moore," Ellen said with a stiff smile plastered on her face, dropping her hand regrettably from Mac's chest. "I have to say I'm surprised to see you working on Christmas."

"Yes, well, some of us take our obligations seriously."

There was the man she'd grown to know and loathe. "You mean like you did to Nathan as one of his groomsmen?" she asked with a sarcastic smirk.

"I know it's easy for that little brain of yours to forget, given how many cells you killed with alcohol recently, but let me remind you I *did* officiate their wedding."

"And yet I don't recall seeing you at the reception much. Gee, I wonder why."

"I'm surprised you could see clearly at all. Let's just say I was in therapy."

"Yeah, okay," Mac said. "Not sure what you two have going on here, but I'm out." He headed toward the door.

"And down for the count by the time my law firm gets

through with you," Jason responded in a quiet but deadly voice, surprising Ellen. She'd never seen him in action and quite frankly hadn't thought he'd had it in him.

Mac paused and sent an amused look in Jason's direction. "Down for the count by the likes of you?" He shot a parting look full of something she couldn't quite identify at Ellen, but then his forehead creased. "Her, maybe," he said before glancing back at Jason and adding, "You? Not likely." Then he headed out the door, calling over his shoulder, "This isn't over, sweetheart."

"I never said it was," she shouted back, then scowled at a gloating Jason as she thought, *Yippee ki-yay, what the hell did I get myself into?*

LATER THAT NIGHT Mac sat in his unmarked car outside of an old brownstone house on a side street in downtown Boston. Ellen's house. He might have left her office, but he hadn't gone anywhere. Snow was out of jail, and while Mac couldn't do anything about it, he wouldn't stop trying to find a loophole.

Ellen Patterson was the key.

She might have said she didn't want anything except to protect her friends, her family. But he wasn't buying it. She was up to something, and he aimed to find out what. She'd walked that Jason Moore guy out of her office to his car and argued with him for a while, until the weasel threw his hands in the air and drove off. Mac didn't like the guy. He seemed way too self-assured and a bit cocky, but that didn't mean Mac couldn't empathize with the dude.

The damned woman was a thorn in his side.

He had to admit he'd never wanted to strangle a woman yet kiss the sense out of her at the same time. She intrigued the hell out of him and infuriated him to the point of wanting to punch something. How could so much dynamite be packed into a body that small? An elf was a good name for her, only she wasn't Santa's helper. He knew trouble when he saw it, but her eyes would be the death of him. A mesmerizing, sparkling green that drew him in and then sucker punched him when he least expected it.

Sinful temptation.

A temptation he would ignore. He didn't need anyone, and he sure as hell didn't need the headache that would undoubtedly accompany getting involved with her. People were overrated. He liked being on his own. Not relying on anyone except himself. It was safer that way. Besides, it didn't matter how the sexy imp made him feel. He could ignore the physical response she stirred within him and focus on the reason he was here.

Revenge.

Picking up his binoculars, he looked through her living room window for the umpteenth time that night. She'd changed into a pair of black yoga pants and a T-shirt with— Christ almighty—no bra. He ground his teeth and reminded himself to stay strong, which was damned hard given the fact that she had the compact body of a gymnast.

She looped a cat with no tail around her shoulders as she disappeared into the kitchen. Then moments later, she reappeared alone to throw on a coat and step outside, carrying a dog with only three legs. Mac ducked down in his seat, peaking just over the edge of the window. She stood there holding the dog's leash until he finished his business, and then she disappeared back inside. Taking off her coat, she curled up in a chair in front of the fireplace and a Christmas tree, then opened a book. She was a people person, who obviously loved the underdog, and she had admitted family meant the world to her.

What the hell was she doing alone on Christmas?

An hour later, a little boy from next door came outside and walked straight toward Mac's car, carrying a mug. The boy looked both ways and then crossed the street, coming to a stop right beside the car. Mac rubbed a hand over his face and sighed, then rolled down his window. The boy didn't say a word, just handed him the mug and then ran back to his house, giggling all the way. How had she spotted him? He must be slipping, but that wasn't surprising, given the effect she had on him.

Mac read the note attached to the Mug.

Hey, MacGruff...

Why don't you put us both out of our misery and come inside? If not, your loss. Here's something to warm those hunky bones of yours.

Elfish Ellen

WHAT THE HELL did that mean? Mac sat there, staring at his mug of black coffee. More importantly, what in the world was he going to do about it?

CHAPTER 3

ELLEN ANSWERED the knock on her door with a grin of satisfaction on her face. She'd hoped the pain-in-the-ass-but-undeniably-gorgeous cop would take the bait. Spending Christmas alone was a lot harder than she'd thought it would be. She didn't know how he did it every year. She'd decided to put her promise to her friends aside for one night and invite Mac inside so she wouldn't be alone.

She'd spotted him earlier, probably because a part of her had been secretly hoping he'd seek her out, then she'd ignored him for most of the evening. It had been thrilling knowing he was out there, watching, waiting. That's why she'd opted to go without a bra. She was bored and lonely and a small part of her had to admit it was fun messing with McMuscles. Not to mention, no matter who he was or what her mission was, she couldn't deny he was hot enough to melt the snow off the North Pole.

"You can't write me a note like that and send it with coffee," Mac said, thrusting the cup back into her hands with a scowl on his ruggedly handsome face. "I'm gonna need something a bit stronger than this."

Ellen laughed. "Don't mind me. That's just the way I talk." She shrugged. "You'll get used to it." Stepping back and opening the door wide, she said, "Come on in, MacGruff, and take a load off."

"You're killing me, you know." He pulled his gaze up from the front of her shirt and stepped inside. Kicking off his boots and coat, he made a beeline for the fire, rubbing his hands in front of the warmth. It was freezing out, yet he'd sat there for hours with his car off, spying on her. He had to be cold.

"Making you suffer was the point." She headed for the kitchen, set the cup in the sink, and then grabbed the bottle of honey Jack Daniels and two glasses. Coming to a stop behind him, she said, "Sit."

He turned around and eyed her warily then took a seat on the couch. "Nice place. It suits you. Small yet oddly intriguing."

"Thanks, I think." She laughed. "Will this do?"

"Whiskey, neat," his voice rumbled. "You're an enigma, woman."

"It's my job to keep you guessing. Call it payback because you certainly are a pro at making people wonder what you're all about."

"And that would be *my* job."

"I take it you're off duty?" She poured them both a drink, set the bottle on the coffee table, and curled up on the couch beside him.

He took one look at her, tossed back his drink in a big gulp, and then responded, "Yeah. Considering I worked all day, I'd say the evening's mine."

"Good," she said, then threw back her own drink without so much as a wince.

His eyelids closed halfway as he eyed her curiously. "You baffle me."

"Isn't that the point of a woman?"

"What's this about, Patterson?"

Deciding she was through playing games, she answered him. "A truce, for tonight anyway." She winked. "And not wanting to be alone on Christmas, Johnson." She held up her glass, and he poured them both another and then clinked his to hers in silent understanding.

This time they both sipped rather than chugged. For the next hour, they drank whiskey and talked about anything and everything. The holidays had a way of doing that to people. They discussed their careers, their hobbies, movies and books they liked...anything except the personal stuff, which was what Ellen truly wanted to know. She suspected he did as well, even though he probably wouldn't admit it. He was just as much an enigma to her. Getting to know him better probably wasn't a good idea, given they were on opposite sides. Yet no matter how hard she tried to keep her distance, there was something about him that drew her in.

"So why *are* you alone on Christmas?" he finally asked softly, indicating Ellen was right. He was curious about her, more than he probably even realized. "This doesn't seem like your normal M.O."

"It's not, believe me," she answered honestly. "I'm one of six kids."

His eyes widened, and she saw small flecks of gold sparkling throughout the rich chocolate brown. "Wow," was all he could get out.

"Yeah," she said with a laugh. "Normally, I love it. But this year was rough. First Nathan and Samantha got married, and now Amber and Kip are engaged. All of my siblings are married. I feel like I'm the old maid of the group." She blinked down at her glass and thought, *Stupid alcohol.* "I don't know, I guess I just wasn't up for the lectures this year," she finally added. "I thought being alone with Flasher and Gimpy would be enough."

"Excuse me?" He eyed her curiously with his lips twitching in the most adorable way.

She tore her gaze away and locked eyes with his as she licked her own lips, which quickly removed the smile from his mouth as his eyes focused on her tongue, sending heat to all the right places. She cleared her throat before speaking.

"Flasher is the cat I rescued after I found her with her tail cut off, and Gimpy is the dog I adopted. No one wanted him because he only has three legs. Can you believe that?" She shook her head in disgust, and Mac stared at her with a look of wonder and admiration and something that made her mouth water. "What's wrong?"

"Not a damn thing," he said, clearing his own throat. "You're, uh, just not what I expected I guess."

"Is that a good thing or a bad thing?" *Super stupid alcohol!* She hated sounding insecure.

"An amazing thing, to be frank," he said. "Yet you scare the hell out of me."

His honesty took her by surprise, and just like that her traitorous heart melted. He scared her too, but she wasn't about to admit that, so she asked, "And why are *you* alone on Christmas?"

"You know why," he said, but his usual heat was missing.

"Just because you don't have a biological family doesn't mean you can't have a family of your own," she pointed out logically. "But you won't let anyone in, will you?"

He swirled the whiskey around in his glass and stared into the fire for a long time before answering. "It's easier this way."

"You mean less painful," she said, knowing exactly how he felt.

His gaze met hers. "Yeah."

"I do the same thing, you know."

His brow puckered. "What do you mean?"

She shrugged. "I don't let people in," she said.

"From what I've seen, you are a total people person with plenty of friends. You light up a room and make everyone around you smile. You have a great family. Even if they drive you crazy, they obviously still love you. Cherish that."

"I do cherish it, but why do you think I'm still single?" she asked, pressing her lips together to stop the flow of words, but the Captain she'd had earlier and the Jack she was having now were betraying her by loosening her lips. "I mean, I don't let *guys* in. Like you, I'm afraid to get hurt. So, I take what I can get and then walk away, acting like I don't care, but I really do. I just don't want to get hurt when they realize I'm not enough for them. And they will. They always do." Dammit, why couldn't she shut up?

"Then they're fools," he said so quickly and with such passion, she sucked in a breath, staring wide-eyed at him, only this time it wasn't an act. "Ellen," he said firmly, reaching out and caressing her cheek as though he couldn't help himself. "I'm not one of them. I'm good at my job, and it doesn't take me long to size people up. I know how amazing you are, even though you try to hide it. That's why I won't just take what I can get and then walk away, because it's not fair to you, no matter how much I want you."

"You want me?" she asked, under the spell of his words.

"Ellen, don't," he said, swallowing hard, and his Adam's apple bobbed.

"Don't what?" she asked, staring at his lips that looked so scrumptious displayed in the middle of his short beard.

She'd felt connected to him from the moment she first laid eyes on him. Sparks had flown from the second she'd talked to him. And now after one lonely evening of baring their souls, she felt like she'd known him forever. Her friends were right. He was dangerous, and she was in big trouble.

"Don't tempt me." He clenched his teeth. "It's been a long ass day, and frankly, I don't know if I have the willpower to resist you, baby."

"Baby?" she asked on another breathy whisper, ignoring the warning signals blaring through her brain.

He squeezed his eyes shut for a moment, and then corrected, "Miss Patterson."

"Too late," she said and proceeded to impulsively straddle him before he could do anything about it.

His eyes sprang open. "God, woman, what the hell are you doing to me?" he asked, grabbing her hips to still her. "This is *not* a good idea. You and I both know that. We are on opposites sides of an investigation. Nothing good can come of this."

She cupped his cheeks with her hands and stared deeply into his wary eyes, wanting to be selfish, if only for tonight. "I don't give a damn about this case or anyone else. It's Christmas, MacGruff. Tonight is about you and me. Period. Screw everyone else. Reality will return soon enough. What do you say?"

He didn't say anything, just pulled her down to him and kissed the sense right out of her.

* * *

MAC COULDN'T BELIEVE he was kissing and caressing Ellen Patterson, something he never thought would happen. It was Christmas. The day he hated most in this world, and yet this stubborn, hard-headed, amazing woman giving him such a gift. He should stop. He had to stop. If he didn't, he could jeopardize everything he'd been working for. A lifetime spent trying to take down the Snows. Yet here was one of their own, tempting him beyond all reason, and he didn't give a damn.

He had to have her.

He stripped off his shirt and then did the same to hers as he stared at the most firm, perky breasts he'd ever seen. They were perfect. God damn, but *she* was perfect. And he hadn't lied. That scared the hell out of him. He never should have gone inside. He slid his palms up her sides and cupped her breasts, tweaking her nipples, and she nearly came undone on his lap. His body stirred, growing harder than he had ever remembered. She wasn't his. He could never hope someone like her could be his. But for tonight, he could pretend.

Pulling her to him, he took a nipple in his mouth and sucked hard.

Throwing back her head, she screamed out his name. Nothing had ever sounded so good. Then she ran her dainty hands over his buzzed head, down his shoulders, and across his torso, touching every inch of his skin as though she couldn't get enough of him. She kissed his tattoos almost like she worshipped him, but he wasn't foolish enough to believe in that. He would simply cherish the gift she was giving him and forget what was normally the worst time of the year for him.

Bringing her face back to his, she took a moment to stare deep into his eyes before kissing him hard. She thrust her tongue into his mouth, and he was a goner. Faster than she could blink, he had her on her back and pulled off her yoga pants. God in heaven, she hadn't worn underwear either. His mouth went dry as he stared down at the perfection beneath him. Her skin was so pale and smooth and perfect. He ran his palm between her breasts, down her flat stomach, and finally to cup her sex. She was so hot and warm and his. A longing more powerful than any he'd ever felt hit him hard. God dammit, he wanted her to be his for real, and that was just plain crazy. It had to be the alcohol, or the day, or something. His hand stilled.

As though reading his mind, she reached up and traced the trust tattoo on his ribs, and then looked deep into his eyes with the same longing and possession he felt. She wanted him as much as he wanted her. He had to remember this was only for tonight. She had even said so. He relaxed and stood, slipping off his jeans, and grew even harder at her look of appreciation. She reached out and cupped him just as possessively, and he nearly came undone in her hand. He joined her on the couch, laying down carefully between her legs so he wouldn't crush her. Pressing his lips to her ear, he murmured words of endearment and appreciation.

He took a moment to trace her mouth with his tongue. Feel the shape of her lips. Taste the sweetness of her skin, then he parted her lips and slipped his tongue inside. She met his with her own and explored every inch of his mouth as well until he thought he would explode. This was a woman who knew what she wanted and wasn't afraid to go after it. He didn't have to play games or guess at what she liked to try to please her. She was so expressive it was both refreshing and exhilarating. He couldn't take much more, or he would explode.

"Baby, let me in," he whispered, adding with a vulnerability he rarely exposed, "please."

That was it. The magical word apparently, because she opened like a flower and gave herself to him completely. He hooked her leg with his arm, pulling it up high and positioned himself in the perfect spot. He hadn't even entered her yet when she bucked her hips and took him inside her with a groan. He nearly lost it as he thrust deep inside the folds of her womb.

She cried out and bit his shoulder. God she was beautiful. He swept his hand over her hair, cupping the back of her head and plunging his tongue deep inside her to the rhythm of his thrusts. She matched him thrust for thrust, wrapping her other leg around his hip and over his butt, pulling him tighter to her. He'd never felt so complete, so one with someone before, but he refused to think about what that might mean. For once in his life, he was determined to think of himself and accept the gift that was being offered, damned the consequences.

Rolling to his back, he took her with him, thrusting deeper with her on top. She looked like a goddess: beautiful, powerful, and in control. How could any man not want to make her his own? She was stunning to watch, and a part of him never wanted this night to end, but he knew that it would. It had to. She rode him hard, and all thoughts left his mind as he lost it, shouting her name as she joined him with a cry and then fell down on his chest.

Mac pulled the blanket from the back of her couch down over them and just held her with all the lights off except for the Christmas tree and the glow from the fireplace. A small smile crept across his face, and he knew he would think of this every Christmas from here on out. Stroking her back until they both fell asleep; his last coherent thought was...

Maybe then his heart would break a little less.

CHAPTER 4

THE NEXT DAY Ellen sat at the table in the board room of Creative Creations, barely listening to their plans for a big New Year's Eve bash for all of their clients. The coward had left her in the wee hours of the morning, afraid to face the truth in the light of day. What happened between them had been amazing. Special. A life-changing miracle.

They were meant to be together!

It was crazy. They barely knew each other yet it felt like they were soul mates. Like they'd known each other before, like maybe in another life. All she knew was he completed the half of her heart that had always been missing. She'd been with plenty of men and had believed it was them who didn't want her. The truth is she was the one who didn't want them.

Because they weren't *him*.

No other man had ever made her feel this way. Now she knew how Samantha and Amber felt, but she couldn't tell them. They were counting on Ellen to sort this whole mess out and make Mac cease and desist in his efforts to destroy both Nathan's and his father's lives. Now that Ellen knew

Mac, she knew for certain he would never quit. His wounds were too deep and his need for revenge too strong. Dammit, she was an idiot to have fallen for him. The stubborn scrooge wasn't willing to let her help him, when she knew better than anyone how much he needed Nathan. He needed a family.

Even if he didn't need her.

"Earth to Ellen, where have you been all morning?" Amber said from beside her, looking tall and strong and happy.

Ellen blinked, coming out of her deep haze and gazing at Amber and Tina, the only two people left in the room. "Sorry, last night was rough."

"I heard," Amber said with a frown.

"Y-You did?" Ellen squeaked. Was she that obvious? Had she made a crazy 911 call to her friends that she didn't remember? Hey, it had happened before, which stood to reason it could happen again. Crap, she needed to start acting like herself again. Love made you stupid. Well, love and alcohol, anyway.

New Year's resolution: stop drinking immediately!

"Your mother called me when you wouldn't answer your phone. I can't believe you didn't spend Christmas with them. That's so not like you. It must have been awful being alone on Christmas." Amber studied her with concern. "What's going on with you? You've been acting funny ever since Sam's wedding."

"Nothing, really, and it wasn't that bad," Ellen replied with relief on a whoosh of laugh. "I've just been a little blue since Sam is now married and you're engaged."

"Why?" Tina asked, barely glancing up from her tablet. "You've got an amazing career. Who needs anything else?"

"That's just because you haven't met the right man yet," Amber replied. "I used to feel the same way, Tina. Ask Ellen."

"It's true," Ellen said. "That's why I'm blue. I've seen how happy both Sam and Amber are. I'm a little bummed I can't have that for myself, but mostly I just don't want things to change our friendship."

"Nothing is going to change our friendship." Amber relaxed and smiled with sympathy. "I still think you should give Jason a chance," she said. "Ask him to be your date at the New Year's Eve bash. Sam and Nate will be back from their honeymoon, and Kip and I are going. You *have* to bring a date."

"Why? I'm not. Is Jason that lawyer who came in yesterday?" Tina looked up fully, her interest finally peaked. "He's hot."

"He's annoying," Ellen responded with a snort. "You go with him. I prefer men like … um, anyone but him." She looked away from Amber's suspicious gaze.

"You're not thinking of getting messed up with Detective Johnson, are you?" Amber asked, nailing Ellen with a firm glare.

"What? No." She huffed, trying to sound like her old self. "Why would you ask?"

"Oh, just because you're an open book. I could tell you were thinking of him, and your face lit up the minute his name was mentioned. You got all flustered," Amber said, and Tina went back to not paying attention.

"That's because Mac flusters me," Ellen said honestly. "You have no idea how hard it is to find out what he's up to and get him to back off of Alexander Snow."

"Mac is it? Right," Amber said with a serious tone. "You have a huge heart, but this is one stray who can't be saved."

Ellen scoffed. "Please. It's me we're talking about. Yes, I might want to help him, but I don't do relationships. You know that."

"Uh huh, and yet something is different about you. Kip and I can intervene at any time. Just say the word. Honey, I don't want to see you get hurt, and guys like Mac have hurt written all over them."

Too late, Ellen thought, but said, "I'm fine. Everything's good. Trust me." She honestly didn't know who she was trying to convince: Amber or herself.

MAC HAD BEEN TAILING Alexander Snow all over Boston. It was a cold and snowy day. The kind that made him wish he was still curled up in front of the fire with the crazy woman who had stolen his heart. All the more reason to have bailed when he did. Focusing on ruining Alexander Snow was what he did best.

The man had met with his attorneys and then a few clients. He was the president of Snow Enterprises, a large import/export company that shipped and received goods out of Boston Harbor. Mac had been watching them for years, waiting for him to slip up. When a tip had come in from an informant, Mac had taken great pleasure in making the drug bust and tainting his company. The fact that Snow had signed off on the shipment only sweetened the pot. And the reality that he was an asshole and a deadbeat dad was enough to make Mac want to see him get life without parole. It would never happen, but one could dream.

Or in Mac's case obsess for the better part of his life.

Snow was back at his office, and Mac had been sitting outside for the past hour, watching and waiting. He didn't believe for a minute that the signature was forged or that Snow hadn't known about the cocaine. He had to slip up sometime, and when that happened, Mac would be ready. The only problem with waiting was it gave a man time to think. And think he did. About the dynamic woman who had driven him crazy, grabbing hold of his heart and refusing to abandon his thoughts.

He hadn't wanted to leave her this morning, but he'd gotten a tip from one of his informants that Snow was on the move. He didn't have the heart to wake her when he left, and a part of him could admit he was afraid to face her after what they had shared. Making love to her had been the best goddamned thing he'd ever experienced, and the stupidest most asinine thing he'd done to date. He knew she'd never be happy with a guy like him.

The problem was she'd brought him to heaven and ruined him for anyone else.

Nope, leaving might not have been the right thing to do, but it sure as hell was the smartest. He was in over his head when it came to her, and he was man enough to admit it. As long as he remained focused on his goal of making his old man pay, he would be fine. He would be satisfied. He would finally be fulfilled. He frowned. Now that he was this close, why didn't he feel more of a sense of elation?

A man left the building and got in Alexander's car, the driver driving off. Mac couldn't be sure who it was so he started his own car and was just about to leave. A movement through the window of the office caught his attention.

"What the hell?" he muttered, shutting off his unmarked vehicle and making his way over to the building under the cover of darkness. Someone was breaking in. Either that or Snow hadn't really left and was inside destroying what evidence there was to prove his guilt. Mac focused, his mind on nothing but his mission, until he reached the entrance.

The door was locked.

Whomever was inside must have the alarm code. Lucky for him, his informant had the code as well. Mac had never expected to have to use it. He wanted Snow behind bars, but he never thought he'd have to risk his job to do it. And code or not, using the code still involved breaking the law, especially since he didn't have a warrant since the place had already been searched. His obsession got the best of him as he quickly made his way inside and crept along the hall until he reached Alexander's office. The building was deserted, other than a small flashlight glowing from beneath the closed door.

As quietly as he could, he opened the door and slipped inside. Not making a sound, he tiptoed over to Snow's desk, pulled out his gun, and said, "Freeze!"

An ear-piercing scream blasted him, and the next thing he knew he was flat on his back with a banshee dressed all in black sitting on his chest. The banshee popped him in the nose, and he saw stars. He blinked, grabbing his nose as his jaw fell open. He snapped it shut and ground out, "No fucking way!"

* * *

"Mac?" Ellen sputtered, lowering her clenched fists and cupping his cheeks to stroke his beard. He looked amazing and felt amazing and she wanted to cry and kiss him at the same time. But then she remembered that he'd pissed her off. "What the hell are you doing, scaring me like that?"

"I think you broke my nose," he growled, looking at her with such a fierce expression, yet he didn't fool her. She knew the real him. He was all bark and no bite. "You mind?" he ground out.

Two could play at this game of indifference. She climbed off his chest and grabbed the tissues on the desk, thrusting them out to him. "Here. You're bleeding."

"Well, this is embarrassing." He sat up and grabbed the box from her, covering his nose with a wad. "I'm twice your size."

She rolled her eyes. "Get over your ego, babe." She thrust her finger at him. "It's your fault anyway."

"You're shitting me. My fault?" His dark brown eyes widened on either side of the bloody tissue covering his nose. "How the hell do you figure that?"

"I don't shit anyone, MacGruff," she snapped, crossing her arms and sitting cross-legged in front of him. Screw indifference. She was still pissed, and he was about to find out how much. "It's not my fault you're an idiot. You've had me on an adrenaline rush since I met you, then you push me over the edge last night, only to disappear on me this morning. To say I'm a little amped up is putting it mildly."

"Gee, ya think?"

She scowled. "You're not helping your case, there spanky."

"And you're not helping yours," he boomed. "I left because I got a call from my informant that Snow was on the move."

"Oh," she said with less bite, feeling a little mollified, but then he had to go and keep talking, ruining everything.

"I know why I'm here," he growled. "To see that justice is done." He stabbed his finger in her direction. "What I want to know is why the hell you're here?"

"You thought you'd get out of seeing me again anytime soon, I know," she said, and he looked away, unable to deny her claim. "You aren't going to let this thing with Snow go, are you?" she asked softly. "Even though his employee has confessed to being the one who forged his signature for the shipment and verified Snow's claim that he knew nothing about the drugs."

"I *can't* let it go," Mac replied just as softly, while looking at anything but her. "He hasn't paid enough."

"That's what I thought you'd say." She sighed. "But tell me…haven't *you* paid enough?"

He took a full minute, staring at the floor and regulating his breathing, then finally replied, "I don't know what you're talking about."

"Yes you do, dammit!" she said, punching him on the arm.

He grunted but didn't stop her.

They could have been so good together if he hadn't been so afraid to let her in. He had no idea she would have done anything for him. She swallowed, moistening her dry throat and squashing her emotions as she replied, "You said so yourself. You have no life, and it isn't because of him. It's because of your *obsession* with him. Admit it. I came close to getting through to you, and that scares you. So you did what you do best and pushed me away while you still could."

He looked her in the eye for a brief moment, and she saw all that he was hiding. It killed her not to shake some sense into him, but he had to want this as much as she did. If he didn't fight for what they had, then it wouldn't be worth anything, so she sat back and did nothing.

He finally replied, "Like I said, you don't know what you're talking about."

"Like hell I don't," she snapped, against her better judgment, rendering him speechless. She couldn't help herself. It was such bullshit. She knew in her gut he felt the same way she did. He wouldn't take a chance and admit it. Tell her how he felt and pray like hell she felt the same way back. The sad thing was he would never know that she truly did.

"You can't look me in the eye and tell me last night didn't mean something to you," she finally responded. "I know it did. I *felt* it. I know you did too. That's why I came here. I wanted to prove once and for all that Snow is innocent. Maybe not innocent of what he did to you, and even to Nathan, but innocent of anything illegal. You have to let this go for there to be any room in your life for me."

Mac's face lost all expression and a blank mask covered his features as he said, "I will never let this go."

And that pretty much told her all she needed to know. He didn't have room for her. Plain and simple. End of discussion. End of relationship. Story of her life.

She started to get up, feeling like her world had been cut out from under her completely. He grabbed her around the waist and pulled her to her feet as he stood beside her. She should have known the only way she could ever beat him was with the element of surprise. He was much bigger and stronger and tougher. She didn't stand a chance against him.

"What are you doing?" she asked, so angry with him she could cry.

"You don't think you're getting off that easily, do you?" his low, gruff voice rumbled from deep in his chest, sounding more angry than necessary.

"For what, caring about you? Believe me, I get it. Big mistake." Her voice broke, and she could have kicked herself.

She saw him wince, looking as pained as her but fighting it for all he was worth as he said, "For breaking and entering. It's against the law, sweetheart."

"I didn't break anything." She thrust her chin in the air and tried to pull away from him to no avail. "I had a code."

"Which you stole, so it's still illegal."

"Not if the man's daughter-in-law gave it to me, you big hairy ape." She couldn't believe he was doing this to her. What on earth did he have to gain? "I'm pretty sure you did the same thing. Maybe I should arrest *you*."

"That does it." He bent low and lifted her over his shoulder, bottoms up, heading for the door as though this had been his plan all along.

She yelped, grabbing him around the waist even though he had a firm grip on her. "What do you think you're doing?"

He slapped her on her bottom. "Locking you up for your own good."

She gasped and then swatted him back. "And what exactly does that mean?" she sputtered, in shock at what he was actually doing, which didn't make a lick of sense.

"That means, you stubborn frustrating woman are under arrest," he said with conviction. "House arrest."

"Who's house?"

"Mine," he stated firmly and then proceeded to carry her out the door.

CHAPTER 5

"Don't look at me that way," Mac said to Ellen as he set her on his massive four-poster, king-sized bed and locked her up with his favorite pair of handcuffs. "You left me no choice. You made me do it." And damned if she didn't make him want to do a whole lot more. He clenched his fists to keep from touching her.

"You're crazy," she countered, eying him warily. "I didn't make you do anything. I think you're sick and twisted and like this sort of thing. Turning a woman inside out and then punishing her when she doesn't do what you want."

"And what exactly did I want you to do?" he asked quietly, removing her dark coat and boots. She wore tight black jeans and a snug black sweater that hugged her curves in all the right places. He swallowed hard, ignoring the way she made him feel.

"Leave you alone," she answered with a raw, honest tone. "Let you slip away with the light of day and pretend that you didn't just change my life forever and then ruin it completely."

"It was powerful, I'll give you that, but it was also the day.

Christmas. It was hard for us both. It stands to reason we'd get caught up in the moment," he said, not quite looking her in the eye as he adjusted her handcuffs, making sure they weren't too tight. The last thing he wanted to do was hurt her more than he already had. "We both knew what this was from the start."

"True," she wrapped her legs around him, lightning quick, and drew him down on top of her, "but neither one of us could have predicted how we would feel after making love."

His heart skipped into overdrive. Grinding his teeth, he closed his eyes against the throbbing in his loins pressed tight and snug against her center. Opening his eyes slowly, he looked at her heavy-lidded, addictive green gaze and said, "Don't, sweetheart. Not tonight."

"Why?" She stared at his lips that hovered only an inch above hers.

"Because I have a job to do." He rubbed his thumb across her bottom lip and cursed softly.

"And that will always come first, won't it?" she asked, her throat sounding clogged with tears. "Your job. Your *obsession*."

His gaze snapped to hers, and he bit back a louder curse as her eyes filled with real tears. "Unfortunately, yes. I won't ever lie to you. It's all I know."

"And it will ruin you."

"Probably so." He traced her features with his gaze, memorizing them, fighting back the words his heart wanted to say, only to say instead, "It's something I have to do."

"Then go." She turned her face away and unlocked her legs from around him. "Whatever. I can't help you if you don't want to be helped."

"I'm not worthy of your help. It's better for us both if you accept that now. I'm no good." He kissed her softly on the cheek, and she turned her face into him, pressing her lips to his as though she couldn't stop herself. She smelled amazing, like vanilla and cinnamon, all warm and full of hope. And she tasted like heaven warring with sinful decadence. He groaned and deepened the kiss, swirling his tongue around hers, and then he pulled away in desperation before he did something stupid.

"I lied," she pleaded in barely more than a whisper. "I don't want you to go. You *are* good. You're perfect for me just the way you are. Please stay with me."

He pulled away from her, not trusting himself to speak. Kissing her once softly on her stomach, he left her side while he still could, turning his back to her as he walked away.

"You're a fool, you know," she called after him.

He hesitated at the threshold, believing every word. He was a fool, a damn fool, but there was nothing he could do about it. He'd hurt her enough. What her eyes didn't say, the slight hitch to her voice confirmed. Mac didn't dare look at her, didn't dare speak for fear his own voice would give her something to cling to and that would be wrong.

The destruction of Alexander Snow had been his life's goal. The goal was finally within reach and Mac would stop at nothing to see it through, even if that meant giving up the best thing that had ever happened to him.

* * *

AN HOUR LATER, Ellen was free. She was double jointed, that's why gymnastics had come so easily to her when she was young. Getting free from Mac's handcuffs hadn't been all that difficult, especially since he'd left them loose so he wouldn't hurt her. Ironic since his handcuffs were the last thing that would hurt her. His pulling away was the devastating part.

He'd shut her out, and that was the worst thing of all. She felt like a stranger to him after all they'd been through. This mission was no longer about proving herself to her friends. They would be just fine without her. This was about loving a man and wanting to give herself to him more than ever before, only to have him reject her. This one hurt more than she'd ever thought it could.

Well, she was done.

She was through with putting her heart on the line when it was obviously not welcome. Through with shedding tears for yet another man who didn't care. Through with loving and thinking someone might actually love her back. She would do what she set out to do and prove Snow innocent, and then she would move on with her life and never look back.

And the first step in making that happen was working with Jason.

Her car was still parked down the street from Snow's office. She'd used the code Sam gave her to sneak in and check things out before Mac had shown up. Just like Alexander had said, she didn't find any records proving he was involved with importing illegal drugs. His employee had acted on his own, but Mac would never rest until he had proof.

That's where Jason came in.

If Ellen could at least find proof with Jason's help, then Mac would have to let his obsession with Snow go. He might not like it, might hate her for it, but at least she would have helped her friends. They were the only people who mattered now. She made her way on foot until she came to a place with a phone. It was dark and cold and she didn't want to walk alone all the way back to Snow's office. She called Jason, and it didn't take him long to come pick her up, no questions asked, which had surprised her.

He pulled up by the curb, and she hopped inside, shivering. He took one look at her, and she thought for sure he'd have some sarcastic comment on how bad she looked. Instead, he said, "Wanna go get a drink? You look like you could use one. I know I sure as hell could. It's been a crappy day."

"You know what?" She looked at him in a new light. "A drink sounds great. I think it's time we had a serious talk."

"I'm all ears."

Two days later Mac headed to the precinct. His captain had called an emergency meeting with him. He hadn't seen or heard from Ellen in two days. Not since he'd spent that last evening trying to pick up Snow's trail to no avail. Returning to his apartment, he'd anticipated teaching Ellen a lesson, but she was gone. He hadn't been surprised, really. She was resourceful and kept him on his toes at every turn. That was one of the things he liked best about her.

He'd planned to let her go anyway. The only reason he'd locked her up in the first place was to keep her from interfering in his investigation if only for a couple hours. That and the fact that he'd fantasized about having her handcuffed to his bed and hadn't been able to resist seeing that played out. He was going to miss having her around.

Hell, he already did.

He climbed out of his car and a cold blast of icy air hit him hard. It was going to be a bitch of a day; he could already tell. Blinking through the sleet pelting him in the face, he jogged inside the police station. He shook the snow off his black leather coat and made his way to the back, nodding hello to several officers along the way. A few people gave him funny looks, while others avoided him. The loud buzz of conversation lowered to a quiet hum. People were acting strange. Something was up. And the way no one would directly meet his gaze made him realize that *something* had to do with him.

He rapped on Captain Scott's door as he said, "It's Detective Johnson, Captain."

"Come in, Detective, and close the door behind you," his captain responded gravely from somewhere inside.

Mac opened the door and started to walk through then froze in his tracks. "What the hell is he doing here?" he asked, narrowing his eyes at Jason Moore who stood on the other side of his captain's desk, wearing a steel-grey power suit with a folder in his hands.

"He's with me," said a voice Mac would recognize anywhere.

He whipped his head to the side and blinked. "Ellen?" Her angry green gaze shot straight through his heart.

She had on a sharp blue suit and high heels as she walked with purpose to stand beside Jason, who rested his hand on her shoulder in support of *what* Mac wasn't exactly sure. All he knew for certain was the possessive beast inside of him reared its ugly head, not happy about the united front standing before him. What the hell were they doing here, together no less? Last he'd seen them, they'd acted like they hated each other, yet now they seemed way too chummy for his liking. Not that he had a damn thing to say about it. He'd made that perfectly clear to her.

Still, he ground his teeth and clenched his fists as the beast roared, *Mine!*

"Have a seat, Mac," his captain said.

"Why?"

"Because I said so," the captain said firmly, then softened his tone as he added, "and I have a feeling this might take a while."

Mac sat as far away from Dasher and Vixen as he possibly could and waited while his captain read the folder. Mac stared at Ellen, not taking his eyes off her and ignoring the imbecile beside her, who had the nerve to gloat. When this was all over with, Mac intended to wipe the smug expression off his pretty-boy face permanently. Ellen refused to meet his gaze, sitting ramrod straight and stiff. She looked proud, determined and gorgeous … yet angry, fragile and hurt. Knowing he was the cause just about undid him. As much as he wanted to, he couldn't cave.

Not until he finished what he'd set out to do.

"This is your idea of dealing with this? Of finishing this thing with Snow once and for all?" His captain finally looked up from the folder, and the expression on his face read anger, frustration and disappointment.

Mac frowned. "What are you talking about?"

"Breaking and entering, trespassing without a warrant, kidnapping for Christ's sake." Captain Scott tossed the folder down and scrubbed a hand over his bald head.

Mac's gaze locked on Ellen accusingly. She blinked a few times and a flash of regret swept over her face, but then she masked her expression and raised her chin a notch.

"It's her word against mine."

"They have proof of Snow's innocence. Miss Patterson's testimony that you kidnapped her against her will. Proof of your uninvited presence without a warrant in Snow's office. Your fingerprints, not to mention your blood, were at the scene." His captain looked at Mac's swollen nose.

Mac cursed. She must have gone back to Snow's office with the weasel that night. "Then you have to know hers were there as well. I only went in because I thought someone was robbing the place. She should be in more trouble than me."

"She knows that, but she's made it clear she doesn't care," his captain stated with resignation. "She will gladly take any heat as long as she gets what she wants."

"And that is?"

"You off this investigation," Jason chimed in with relish. "I think it's time you backed off, Johnson. Step aside. You of all people should know your place and where you don't belong." He looped his arm around the back of Ellen's chair. She stiffened a bit but didn't move or speak.

Mac surged to his feet.

"Enough, Detective!" Captain Scott stepped between Mac and Jason faster than Mac had seen him move in years. Good thing because he couldn't be held responsible if he ripped the weasel's throat out. He'd provoked the beast, and he damn well knew it.

"This is bullshit, Captain," Mac growled.

Captain Scott was already shaking his head. "Even if you were justified in entering the office, the mayor won't want any negative press attached to this precinct. It's bad enough you've been after one of Boston's most prominent citizens for years. Snow donates to several charities, as well as this force.

He has for years. Christ, they play golf together." He raised his hands in the air.

Mac gaped at his boss. "You're actually considering granting their ridiculous request?"

"Dammit, MacKenzie!" The captain pounded his fist on the desk. "You've left me no choice. Miss Patterson won't cause any trouble for us or press charges against you if you leave quietly. This might be a good time for you to take a vacation."

Mac looked at Ellen. He didn't even try to hide his feelings. She'd taken away what she knew was most important to him: revenge against the man who had forsaken him and vindication that he was important and worthy to be loved. He'd wanted, no *needed*, for his father to have everything important taken away from him. Just like Mac had experienced. He needed him to suffer and maybe, just maybe, regret his actions and the effect they'd had on an innocent boy.

Now that would never happen because of her.

"You win," he said directly to her. "I hurt you, and you hurt me back, just like you said you would. I hope you're happy." He took off his badge and handed it to his captain.

Captain Scott frowned. "What are you doing? I said take a vacation, not leave the force."

"I quit."

Ellen's mouth fell open on a gasp and she stood.

"Son, are you sure you want to do this? You're a damn good cop."

"Now you won't have to worry about the mayor or the press or this precinct," Mac said sincerely. "You guys are my family, Captain. I would never do anything to hurt that. It's better for all of us if I distance myself."

Ellen took a step toward him, touching his arm and speaking directly to him for the first time. "Mac, don't do this. That's not what I wanted."

"Too late. Moore's right. You don't belong with me. I only tried to do what was in your best interest." He looked down at her hand in pain, then stepped back until her fingers fell away.

He let his gaze meet hers, revealing everything he felt inside. "You took what I wanted most away from me, and the only real family I ever had." He shrugged. "That's nothing new, I just didn't expect it from you." His face hardened, letting the fact that he would never forgive her shine bright in his eyes. "Don't think this is over, sweetheart. I might be off the case officially, but unofficially I'll never stop."

She pressed her lips together and blinked back tears, staring at him helplessly.

He turned around and walked out the door, shutting it and her out of his life for good.

CHAPTER 6

"HE HATES ME," Ellen said, wiping her nose with a tissue. She sat on her couch, with Flasher and Gimpy on either side of her, and cried harder as she stared at the Christmas tree she couldn't bear to take down. The fireplace would remain lit for as long as she could stand it because it reminded her of the night she'd fallen head over heels in love with MacKenzie Johnson aka Detective Scrooge MacGruff.

"He doesn't hate you, sweetie," Amber said, refilling their glasses with wine. She'd dropped everything, leaving her fiancé and wedding plans to rush to Ellen's side the second she had called.

"Honey, he's just hurting, that's all," Samantha said, passing around a box of chocolates and a carton of ice cream. She and Nate had come back from their honeymoon a day early after Amber had called them.

Ellen's friends were the best, which only made her sadder thinking about Mac out there all alone without even his cop family now. It was all her fault. In trying to pay him back for hurting her, she'd destroyed him when he hadn't done anything to deserve it. She was the one who had seduced him when she'd known from the start he wasn't relationship material. He'd even tried to stop her, but she'd been relentless because she'd wanted him so much. She'd actually thought she could change him, but she'd ruined him instead.

And now he hated her.

"You all were right. I never should have gotten involved," she said, sniffling. "Snow didn't need me to fight his battles, and Mac didn't need me to push him into something he wasn't ready for. All I did was cause more trouble, and here you two are once again, bailing me out."

"You have a big heart. It's not in your nature to stand aside and do nothing when someone needs help. That's why we all love you so much." Samantha took a sip of wine, looking thoughtful.

"You're fiercely loyal and protective when you love someone." Amber popped a chocolate in her mouth and chose her words carefully as she chewed. "If Mac can't see that, then it's his loss. You would have given him the world if only he'd let you in."

"Instead, I gave him heartache." Ellen hiccupped, then blew her nose again.

"Heartache's a two-way street, babe," Amber added, grabbing the carton of ice cream. "Looks to me like he gave you some right back."

"Things will get better, El," Samantha said, her voice full of sympathy. "You just have to have faith and believe. I remember not long ago I thought my life was over when Nathan gave me my freedom and let me walk out of his life. And look at me now, happily married."

"I hear that. I thought for sure Kip would walk out of mine

after we were rescued and our fantasy was over," Amber added. "Yet here I stand blissfully engaged."

"We all have issues we have to overcome." Sam grabbed Ellen's hand.

"Yeah, if it's meant to be, then it will be." Amber took her other. "Have patience, but know that whatever happens, you won't be alone. We'll always be here for you."

"I could have all the patience in the world, but you guys don't know Mac like I do. He's incapable of letting it *be*, and I will never love another like I do him. Dammit, what I feared most is finally going to come true," Ellen said, adding with a deep and utter sadness she didn't think she would ever get over, "I'm destined to spend my life alone."

* * *

"You're a hard man to track down," a deep voice said as a man sat down at the bar.

Mac had been at Willy's—a dive not many people knew about—for hours. Great food, cool atmosphere, and bartenders who left you alone. He liked going there because he could be by himself and not run into anyone he knew from work. He laughed harshly in his mind. Not that he had to worry about that these days since he didn't have a job to go to anymore.

"Gotta say I'm surprised you bothered to look," he said without glancing up. He knew exactly who was beside him. His long-lost brother. They not only looked alike, they sounded identical. It was like listening to himself on his answering machine. It always felt weird hearing his voice. This time was no exception.

Nathan ordered a beer and a shot, same as him. After tossing back the shot, he took a sip of beer as though gathering his thoughts. "The old man's not worth it, you know."

Mac stiffened, but only a little. The fight had gone out of him along with the only light in his life that he'd ever had. The light that had betrayed him, sending him into a future full of darkness. "I'm beginning to see that," he responded.

"We're more alike than you realize." Nate sipped his beer again.

Mac grunted. "So I've been told. Forgive me if I have a hard time believing it."

Nate chuckled softly. "God, you remind me of myself not long ago. I spent a lot of years alone, hating dear old dad, trying to get back at him for never being there for me. It sucked being alone. I wish like hell I had known about you."

"Yeah, well, you didn't." Mac chugged his beer.

"But I do now."

Mac slowly lowered the glass to the bar and studied Nathan. It really was unnerving how much they looked alike. Squashing the odd sensation it filled him with, he looked away and finally said, "Your point?"

"I don't know about you, but I'm sick of being alone." Nathan's voice rang with sincerity.

"Says the man who just came back from his honeymoon." Mac snorted. It was more of a defense mechanism than anything because he couldn't handle being tempted with something he'd always longed for. Family.

"You know what I mean. Samantha is amazing, and I'm lucky to have her. That doesn't mean I've stopped wishing I had a brother—which is something I've wished for my whole life, by the way."

"Me too," Mac grudgingly admitted, and then frowned down at his drink. Damned alcohol got him in trouble every time. "Don't think this means I'm going to cry on your shoulder," he added.

"I'd have to punch you if you did." Nate grinned at him just the way Mac had imagined a real brother would, and he couldn't help smiling back a little. "I'm just asking for a chance to be a part of your life," Nate added sincerely.

Mac hesitated for a long moment and then finally said, "I'll think about it."

"Good." Nate finished his beer, setting down enough money for them both, then stood. "While you're at it, you might want to think about letting other people in. Life sucks a whole lot less with the right woman by your side."

A sharp pain that was still way too raw burned through Mac's chest. "Bridges burned are pretty hard to cross."

"That's the great thing about New Year's. You get a do-over." Nate squeezed Mac's shoulder. "Maybe it's time to build a new bridge." Then he left Mac alone to his thoughts, which would trouble him for the rest of the night.

ELLEN STOOD in the lobby of Creative Creations on New Year's Eve, staring in wonder at the fabulous job her team had done in decorating the place. She owed them. She'd been no help whatsoever, blubbering away like a fool, which made her really angry at herself. The place truly looked like a magical wonderland, decked out in sparkly silver and gold, with bells everywhere. They would all count down and when the New

Year hit at the stroke of midnight, they would jingle the bells to signal the start of a brand-new year. A time of new beginnings.

A fresh start.

Not one to stay down, she was through with her pity party. She'd hurt Mac, but he had hurt her too. Her friends were right. If it was meant to be, it would have happened. And since it obviously wasn't going to, then it was his loss for missing out on a lifetime of loving her. She was a damned good catch, and some day, she was determined to make someone a very happy man.

The party was in full swing already. She'd arrived late, finally snapping out of her funk and deciding to go at the last minute. Which meant of course she didn't have anything to wear. After calling literally every contact in her book, they made exceptions because it was her, and they opened their shops after hours.

She felt like a princess, and she'd decided she deserved to feel like a princess every damn day of her life. She didn't need a man to make her happy, she just had to love herself. She studied her reflection in the mirror and smiled wide.

Now, *this* self she was crazy about.

Her dress was a strapless sparkly green that matched her eyes and hugged her gymnast curves, pushing up her cleavage and stopping just above her knees. She'd opted to go without nylons and wore three inch silver heels with a matching clutch. That was the best part of being short. She could wear higher heels than everyone else.

Her diamond necklace and earrings were on loan from her favorite jeweler with the promise she would return them in perfect condition and give them a discount off the campaign she was working on for them. Her hair had been styled by a top salon for free since the campaign she'd just completed for them had tripled their business.

Life was good.

Or at least it would be. A small part of her was still a little sad, but she planned to bury that part with a whole lot of champagne and have fun tonight. Snagging a glass off a passing waiter's tray, she joined her friends by the buffet table.

"You made it," Amber said, looking amazing in a honey-colored mid-calf evening gown as she gave her a big hug.

"Ellen Patterson," Kip said, picking her up in his arms and swinging her around, looking as hot and godlike as ever. "Always a sight for sore eyes."

Ellen laughed the first real laugh she'd had in days and grinned up at him. "Hey there, Captain Yummy. You have any problems with this Amazon, you know where to find me. I've still got a few tricks up my sleeve." She winked at him.

"You know it," he said, high-fiving her.

Amber stared at him with love in her eyes and gratitude, but said, "Trust me, he's gonna need all the help he can get to top me."

"Baby, you can be on top any time you want, just say the word." He took his fiancé in his arms, and she didn't even try to put up a fight.

Ellen smiled happily for them. "Get a room." She laughed. They really were perfect together.

"There's my favorite, peace keeper," Nathan said, coming up behind her and giving her a gallant bow like a true hand-some knight-in-shining-amour.

Ellen grinned as she hugged him. "Nathan, it's so good to

see you." She stepped back and looked him in the eye, which was harder than she thought given how much he looked like Mac. "Hey," she covered her sadness by asking, "you treating my best friend right?"

"You being naughty?" He arched a thick black brow.

"I take it that's a yes then." She winked and then laughed, feeling better by the minute.

"You look fabulous, El," Samantha said, as she wrapped her arms around her. Sam wore a floor-length, periwinkle blue ball gown, looking amazing as usual.

"All this?" Ellen stepped back and swept her hand down her body. "Please, it's just a little something I threw together last minute." She couldn't hide the smirk on her face if she tried, and at the moment, she didn't feel like hiding anything.

They were all dysfunctional and awesome and hers!

"Right." Sam shook her head. "I'm just so glad you came." Her face sobered. "I wasn't sure you would. Are you truly okay?"

"It's all good." Ellen looked them each in the eye, suspecting they could see her sadness because they knew her so well and loving them for it, but wanting to reassure them. "I'm better now, or at least I will be soon. I promise."

"Jason's here," Amber said, pointing over to the bar in a last-ditch effort.

"Jason is actually a much nicer guy than I gave him credit for," Ellen said honestly. "But I'm not ready to move on yet." She actually didn't know if she would ever be, but she would damn sure try. "Besides, I think he and Tina would make a great couple."

"You think so?" Samantha asked, eyeing them both in a

new light judging by the matchmaking spark Ellen saw shining in her eyes.

"I *know* so," Ellen said with certainty. "They are both beautiful, smart workaholics who have no idea what they are missing out on. Lock them up in a room together, and I guarantee sparks would fly."

"Hey, guys, look at the time," Kip said, pointing to the clock. "Grab a drink and a bell. It's almost midnight."

All of them rushed over to the bar except for Ellen. She trailed behind, letting them bask in the excitement of starting their new lives together and all the possibilities that brought along with it. She smiled, truly happy for them, but suddenly regretting coming. She had thought she could easily move on and start over, but the truth was, she'd lied. She wasn't fine and she didn't want to move on, dammit! She didn't want anything new. She desperately wanted what she'd left behind. Her throat clogged tight and her eyes filled with unshed tears.

She had been a fool to come tonight.

The countdown started, and she stood still, watching in silence. Everyone picked up a bell and started to count.

Ten, Nine, Eight...

Ellen took a step back toward the door, suffocating, needing some air.

Seven, Six, Five...

They'd never miss her. She had to leave now while she still could.

Four, Three, Two...

And the only man she wanted to kiss was gone.

One...

Oh, God, she couldn't do this. She turned around to make her escape when someone wrapped his arms around her, swooped down and kissed her like there was no tomorrow. She heard bells as firm lips softened against hers, and her arms slipped around his neck, melting. She had to be dreaming. The first tears spilled over her eyes as she held on tight until he lifted her in the air and pressed her against his chest, never breaking the kiss. She tilted her head to the side and deepened the kiss. He spun her in a slow circle, holding her as though he never intended to let her go. If this was a dream, she never wanted to wake up, because reality sucked without MacKenzie Johnson in her life.

Finally, slowly, he let her slide down the length of his muscular body until her feet hit the ground and she came back to earth. He pulled his head away from hers, but not far, as he said with a voice full of emotion, "Happy New Year, Ellen."

"Is it?" she asked with just as much emotion.

"Very," he said with honest sincerity and a bit of moisture in his own eyes.

"Why? How could it possibly be?" She hiccupped, knowing her nose was red, her eyes puffy, and that she looked a mess, but she didn't give a damn. He was here now, right in front of her. If he was playing with her, he was a dead man.

He ran his hands over her hair and face, his gaze tracing her features like he was memorizing her, worshiping her, and then he stared deep into her eyes. "Because I love you Ellen Patterson. With all my heart. That's enough for me. Just knowing that I *can* love someone. I know I probably ruined any chance I had with you by shutting you out and pushing you away. I was afraid that you would do it to me first, and I couldn't handle that. Now I realize *life* is scary, but loving someone is worth the risk."

"But I cost you everything," she said on a sob of regret, afraid to believe what she was hearing.

"You cost me nothing." He wiped away her tears with his thumbs. "My captain gave me my job back, and someone who's turned out to be pretty important to me made me see that the old man isn't worth it. The only thing I lost was you. I understand if you need time, and I know I have a lot of making up to do, but baby, I can't live without you. I'll wait forever if that's what it takes, but just know I'll never stop loving you."

"You really love me?" she asked in wonder.

"Yes, I do. More than I ever thought possible." His lips twisted into an adorable grin. "Let's just say you're my new obsession. And you know what I do when I'm obsessed. I fight dirty, hold on tight, and never let go."

Her smile came slow and sweet. "I can live with that. You should know by now I like dirty."

"What are you saying?" He looked hopeful yet scared to death.

"That I love you too, MacGruff." She kissed him soundly on the mouth. "Marry me?"

He blinked, startled, then threw back his head and laughed, picking her up once more and spinning her around again. "Yes, my little firecracker. Leave it to you to steal my thunder by asking me first."

"I can think of a few ways you can make it up to me." She whispered in his ear. "But if you throw me over your shoulder again, all bets are off."

He laughed heartily, scooped her carefully into his arms and cradled her close as he carried her out the door to his waiting car. She snagged a bell and let it jingle all the way to his apartment, where she planned to make good use of those handcuffs all night long, locking up his heart and throwing away the key. It belonged to her now, and she didn't plan to ever let it go. *She* was his family, and she planned to spend the rest of her life showing him exactly what that meant.

SLEIGH BELLS RING

CHAPTER 1

"The man makes me crazy!" Amber Evans said from the back of the plush limousine, refusing to drink the complementary top-of-the-line chilled champagne or eat the ridiculously-expensive caviar. She tossed her pin-straight, super-long brown hair over her shoulder and crossed her arms over her athletic frame, feeling like the elephant in the room as usual, next to her friends.

Her best assets were her whisky-colored, almond-shaped eyes and ultra-long lashes. Or so she'd been told. She was fine with her looks, and had even embraced her tall-girl stature; she'd just given up on men not being intimidated by her. And forget about a man ever swooning over her, especially in the presence of Miss Adorable and soon-to-be Mrs. Gorgeous.

"What man doesn't make you crazy?" Her best friend Elfish Ellen Patterson—who was an adorable, petite, short-haired, red-headed, green-eyed pixie—snorted. She sat on one side of the limo, digging into the food with gusto.

A groan came from her other best friend Samantha Darling—a blond-haired, blue-eyed, gorgeous Barbie Doll with curves in all the right places. Samantha leaned back against the opposite seat, sipping her drink and rubbing her temple.

They had known each other forever and had been the Three Amigos for years, working together at a Boston advertising firm, but now Sam was about to get married and change everything. Amber couldn't help feeling like the wicked stepsister, except she loved her Cinderella. She just wished for a fairy tale of her own.

"Don't get me wrong. I'm really happy for you, sweetie," Amber quickly amended, reaching out to squeeze Sam's hand.

She adored both of her friends, and had known Sam since high school. Ellen had come along during college, and the rest was history. Blissfully ending up at the same firm was like spreading the icing on the proverbial cake. But now that Samantha had reformed business tycoon McScroogy Nathan Snow, life as they knew it would never be the same. Amber had known it would change eventually, but she still hadn't quite accepted it. And Caveman Kip Covington wasn't making matters any easier.

"I just can't stand your fiancé's best man. He has to take control of everything," she added.

"You haven't even met him, Amber," Ellen said, after taking a sip of her bubbly and wrinkling her nose while wearing a grin over the fizz. "Give the guy a shot. He could be hot." She wagged her brows. "He sure has good taste, which tells me the man can't be *all* bad."

"Trust me. You can have him." Amber scoffed.

"Don't be ridiculous. Have you seen his picture? He has sexy playboy looks, but he's literally like a seven-foot giant, and I'm a mere five feet tall." Ellen sighed dramatically. "Sadly, it would never work. Besides, you're the maid of honor. He's all yours, babe." She winked.

"He's not *my* anything, and the only reason you don't want him is because you know he's not man enough to handle you and all your wild ways. Besides, I heard he doesn't date. No one is ever good enough for His Highness. I will walk down the aisle with him, and that's it," Amber grumbled. "He could have handled Nathan's bachelor party and left the bachelorette party to me, but no. He had to try to outdo me, like he has in everything else all year long."

"He means well," Sam said. "You would see that if you would ever let yourself get to know him. For my sake as well as Nate's, can't you at least *try* to get along?" Sam asked, wearing a pleading look in her eyes.

Amber felt a twinge of guilt for complaining about the former NBA star, who thought he was God's gift to women and had the cocky attitude to go along with it. She'd be damned if she'd give him the chance to shoot her down like he did countless other women. She read the tabloids. She knew exactly what he was like, because she'd been burned by enough male athletes back in her college volleyball days, just because they couldn't handle that she was as athletic and tough as they were. Frankly, she'd had enough of men in general, and certainly didn't need one to be happy.

"I can't help it—the man has too much time on his hands and not nearly enough to do, other than mess with my life on a daily basis," Amber said, then took a deep breath and counted to ten before adding, "but I'm sorry for upsetting you. I will *try* to get along with him for you, but I'm still not drinking his stupid champagne or eating his nasty caviar." She sat back stubbornly, knowing she sounded like a child, but she couldn't help it. The man brought out the worst in her. She stared at the matching limo in front of them as she added, "In fact, I hope he chokes on them. It would serve him right for showing off. All I can say is that if he tries to mess with me here, then all bets are off and he's going down."

* * *

"THE WOMAN SERIOUSLY DRIVES ME NUTS," Kip Covington growled from the back of the limo the guys were riding in, his head lightly touching the ceiling.

His large frame barely fit in *any* vehicle, but he'd grown accustomed to that over the years. He shook back his shoulder-length, pale-blond curly hair, having opted to leave it loose instead of tying it back in his standard ponytail.

His ex-wife had liked his light gray eyes, but preferred his hair short, so he'd defiantly refused to cut it since the day she'd screwed him over by cheating on him with another player. Much to his surprise most other women preferred his hair long, but he didn't trust any of them. He'd learned the hard way that women only wanted him for his fame and money, so other than satisfying an occasional need, he wanted nothing to do with them. Women were a fickle bunch, and not worth the drama that accompanied them, especially the woman riding in the car behind them. She was the biggest drama queen he'd ever met.

"She's not so bad once you get to know her," Nathan Snow said, still wearing his black suit with his black gelled hair slicked back and black eyes as sharp as ever. He was clean-shaven, but his beard was so heavy, he still sported a five o'clock shadow—something Kip had never had to worry about.

Having come straight from work, Nate still donned his ruthless businessman personality, but the minute he was in his fiancé's presence, he transformed into someone Kip barely recognized. Dressing in color, wearing his hair loose and wavy, and doting on the gorgeous Samantha Darling like a lovesick puppy. It somehow made him seem human, instead of just the cold machine he was known to be. Kip appreciated and had first-hand experience with Nate's savvy business sense. After Kip retired from basketball, Nate helped him open his very successful and profitable romantic getaway ski lodge in Vermont called Snuggler's Nook. Yes, he had to admit he enjoyed this new side to Nate's personality as well. Romance certainly agreed with him.

The only thing Kip didn't envy was Nate's getting engaged, no matter how great Samantha seemed to be. More power to him, but that was something Kip never planned to do again. Too bad Sam's sweetness hadn't rubbed off on her maid of honor, Amazon Amber Evans.

"The stubborn woman doesn't appreciate anything," Kip replied in frustration. "I closed down my lodge so all of us could have it to ourselves for a whole weekend. That's risky business this time of year, but it's something I wanted to do because you and Sam deserve it. The wedding plans are finalized, and there's nothing left to do. This long weekend is exactly what we *all* need before the big day next week. Why can't Amber just accept it, instead of getting all bent out of shape? I wasn't trying to step on her enormous feet that she keeps putting in her mouth with all her childish text messages and e-mails. I was just trying to help."

"Come on, man, you know women," Jason Moore—of Moore and Griswald, Attorneys at Law—said, helping himself to another Manhattan. "They have to be in control of everything, or at least *feel* like they are, in order for them to be happy. Your problem is you've just never learned how to play the game."

He looked like a normal average guy, in his standard brown suit with an average build and average light brown hair and eyes, but that was his strength. People had no clue he was a powerful defense attorney who represented big-name athletes and usually won. That's how Kip had met him. Nate had met him through Kip, and they'd hit it off instantly. Shark recognized shark, and the two had become fast friends. Nate had several powerful friends, just not many he trusted to be his best man and groomsman.

"Oh, I know how to play the game," Kip ground out. "I just don't like games. Never have, never will. Unless they're of the athletic kind and not the mind. My ex certainly played enough mind games to last me a lifetime."

"I'll drink to that." Nate held up his Scotch, and Kip raised his beer.

"To new beginnings and fresh starts," Jason added, raising his own glass.

"Amen." Kip grunted, and they all clinked glasses.

"I don't have to tell you how much this weekend means to Samantha." Nate rested his elbows on his knees, across from Kip. "Do whatever you have to do to slap on that charm of yours and play nice."

But something told Kip getting through this weekend in one piece would never be as easy as that.

* * *

THE LIMOS PULLED up in front of a small but quaint and rustic ski lodge, fully decorated for the holiday season. It was set in a remote area of Vermont, sporting an intimate feel that would cater to young couples in love, or singles looking for love, rather than the massive ski resorts the area was known for. Probably a smart business decision to come up with a niche that nobody else had, but still. Amber stared at the sign, Snuggler's Nook, and rolled her eyes.

The man was something else.

"Okay, ladies, let's hit it," she said at last, dreading finally meeting Caveman Kip face-to-face. They'd dealt with each other several times over the past year, but had never met in person. The sooner they started this awful weekend, the sooner it would be over with; then they would never have to see each other again after the wedding. "It's showtime," she added, her determination ringing out loud and clear.

"Remember," Sam said, with a warning tone in her voice, "play nice."

"To heck with that," Ellen chimed in. "I plan to play dirty. Go big or go home, chicas." She laughed as she bounced out of the limo first in her wrinkled green dress.

Amber could have sworn she heard bells. Sam smiled and shook her head, stepping out of the limo in a much more ladylike fashion in her sharp blue suit, her naughty days long gone as her eyes fixed on her husband-to-be. Amber inhaled slowly, trying to calm the knots in her stomach as she smoothed her fawn-colored pant suit. For some reason she was nervous to meet Kip, which was so unlike her. She was used to being the one to make people nervous, not the other way around. Giving herself a mental order to suck it up and put on her game face, she slid out of the limo with confidence that was short-lived.

Her jaw fell open and she nearly swallowed her tongue as she looked up. Way up, and that had *never* happened before. Kip Covington was enormous. The setting sun streamed down out of a cloudless sky, sparkling off the pristine white snow and spotlighting the man, making his hair look like a glowing halo. He stood a foot above her six-foot-frame, sporting impossibly wide shoulders and the longest arms and biggest hands she'd ever seen.

The magazine pictures didn't hold a candle to what it was like to see him in person. From the top of his pale-blond curly hair—which truly was Playgirl centerfold sexy-as-hell—past his Big and Tall, mouthwatering, silver warm-up suit, clear down to his size twenty-two high-tops. The man could seriously give Shaq a run for his money.

For the first time in her life, Amber felt small and feminine standing before him. He looked like the God of Thunder, Thor. An image of him locking his striking pale gray eyes on hers, then wrapping his muscular arms around her and pulling her in to lower his head and press his full lips against hers, rendered her speechless. She stood there slack-jawed and mute. But then he had to go and speak, which pretty much ruined her moment-of-Kipsanity fantasy.

Thank God! What the hell had she been thinking, lusting after a caveman?

"Amazon Amber in the flesh." His knowing gaze ran over her, making her cheeks flush hot and her spine snap straight. Had she seen a halo? Not a chance with this Neanderthal. Devil horns would be much more accurate, she thought, as he finished with, "Nice to finally meet you, I hope." He held out his enormous hand.

"Charmed, I'm sure I'm *not*, Caveman Kip. And I'll let you know if it's nice by the end of the weekend." She grasped his hand, squeezed tight and shook firmly, which only made his cocky grin spread wider. The rat.

"Holy crap, I barely clear your belt buckle," Ellen blurted. "Hmm. Could come in handy." She tipped her head to the side, studying him, then blinked over Sam's gasp. Ellen looked up, not blushing in the least as she grinned wide and said, "Whoops. Was that out loud?"

Kip laughed a big, hearty, deep boom, then carefully shook Ellen's tiny hand. "Now *you*, I can honestly say it's very nice to meet."

"Likewise, Jolly Blond Giant." Ellen's gaze blatantly ran over every impressive inch of him. "Something tells me getting too close to you could be dangerous to a person's health. You seriously need a warning label, dude."

"And something tells me getting too close to dynamite could seriously burn a person." A wide grin remained on his chiseled face.

"I *have* been known to be a bit explosive." She wagged her brows.

"I don't doubt that at all. I've heard that big things come in small packages." He chuckled.

Amber rolled her eyes. *Good Lord in Heaven.*

"This is going to be a fun weekend." Ellen turned her gaze on the much shorter man standing beside him. "You must be Jason," she said in a flirty voice, then bit her lip.

He looked up from his smart phone and blinked. "Pardon

me? Oh, yes. I'm Jason Moore of Moore and Griswald, Attorneys at Law. And you must be Ellen Patterson."

"Why, yes. Yes, I am," she said in a serious James Bond voice. "Ellen Patterson of Patterson, Evans, and Darling, Advertising Executives at Large."

She laughed... he did not.

"Okey dokey, then," she continued, the teasing note long gone. "Methinks I spoke too soon." She dropped her hand after he refused to shake it, staring at her with an expressionless face. Her sparkle faded as she finished with, "Peachy."

Nathan Snow's forehead formed a deep menacing V, clearly not amused, as he stared at the four of them. After they all squirmed a bit, he turned his attention to Samantha, and everything about him softened. "What do you say we get this party started, darling?" He held out his arm.

She looped hers through his. "Sounds wonderful to me. I for one am more than ready to have a nice, relaxing, *fun* weekend with the people Nathan and I hold most dear." She looked them each in the eye with a no-nonsense expression, her warning abundantly clear. "And I'm sure *everyone* is, as well, since this weekend is supposed to be about Nathan and me, right?"

They each nodded sheepishly. Kip finally stepped forward, giving instructions for his limo drivers to bring everyone's bags inside, and then telling them they were free to go. He turned to Nate and Sam.

"Just so you know, we have this place completely to ourselves. I've even given the lodge staff the weekend off. Rest assured they prepared full meals to get us through, so no one will have to cook, but I thought it might be nice for it to truly be just the six of us. No press, no guests, no staff, just total rest and relaxation, and yes, *fun.*" His gaze shot to Amber briefly, then he said, "If you'll all follow me, I'll lead the way inside."

Of course he would, Amber thought, but didn't dare say anything. Just like with everything else, he'd already started by completely taking over once again. He might have provided the place, but she'd be damned if she'd let him control the whole weekend. Little did he know she had a few plans of her own. She'd show him how fun she could be. Fun with a capital F, but he wouldn't be laughing by the time she got done with him.

CHAPTER 2

THAT EVENING, after a fabulous steak dinner, they all got settled into their rooms. Every room was like a honeymoon suite with a monstrous four-poster king-sized bed, a heart-shaped Jacuzzi, and a wall of windows with a stunning view of the mountain. It was a shame to be staying there without a significant other, but no way would Amber share that bed with Scrooge McDunky.

Changing into her own gold warm-up suit, she headed down to meet up with everyone in the lodge for some after-dinner drinks and fun. No doubt Kip had that planned out as well, but Amber had a mind to put a kink in his plans and let him know he wasn't the only one calling the shots.

The suites were all upstairs and to the sides of the lodge, while on the main floor, the center of the lodge opened up into a great room with cathedral ceilings. A massive fireplace occupied one side of the room, with comfortable couches and chairs scattered about, while a huge bar occupied the other side of the room, with the front of the lodge sporting floor-to-ceiling windows that showcased a stunning view. The biggest Christmas tree Amber had ever seen stood by the window, waiting to be decorated, and a very small part of her softened. Kip must have known about Samantha's love for Christmas, and decorating the tree was her favorite part.

Nathan's hair was now gel-free, loose and wavy, and he wore a pair of dark jeans with a burgundy sweater that looked cashmere soft. He sat on one of the couches, while Samantha sat on his lap in a pair of her own jeans that displayed her curves perfectly, along with a periwinkle silk blouse that revealed her generous assets and brought out the stunning blue of her eyes. They looked so happy and in love as they cuddled while admiring the tree. Amber could practically see the creative wheels spinning in her best friend's brain over how she would decorate it, making Amber not want to intrude.

Ellen, on the other hand, had no clue, as she bounced into the room in a pair of black yoga pants, with a fitted teal T-shirt and matching headband that accented her cute pixie haircut. No one could help smiling when Ellen entered a room. Except maybe Jason, who was a decent-enough-looking guy, but boring and all business, twenty-four seven. He sat by the bar with his nose buried in his smart phone again, while sipping a martini. His idea of changing into something more comfortable had been to don a pair of khakis and white button-down shirt. Ellen took one look at him, reversed direction, and plopped down next to Nate and Sam.

Wanting to beat Kip to the prime spot in front, Amber started walking in their direction. Of course Kip had to enter at that moment, still wearing his same silver warm-up suit, since he lived in casual every day. The only thing he'd changed was he'd pulled back his long hair into a short ponytail at the base of his neck, giving him a rakish pirate appeal.

Amber frowned. Where had that come from? She didn't want to think of him as rakish or anything else even remotely positive. He was a caveman. Bossy and arrogant with no manners. As long as she remembered that, she'd be just fine.

Kip's gaze met hers. Something flashed in his eyes, and she set her jaw. Game on! They both took off practically running to get to Nate and Sam first. She beat him by a single step and let out a "Ha!"

Everyone looked at her strangely, so she swept her long hair over her shoulder and corrected, "I mean, hey." She waved, taking the spot right in front triumphantly.

Kip arched a blond brow at her and just grunted. He looked across the room at Jason, and opened his mouth as if to say something.

"Hey, Jason, why don't you come join us," Amber beat Kip to the punch, while shooting him a smug grin.

Kip stared at her hard for a minute, and then countered, "Hold up, Jason. I'll get a drink order, and you can help me carry them back." He smirked at Amber, and they both blurted at the same time, "What does everyone want?"

Sam and Nate just stared at each other and shook their heads.

Jason looked up confused.

Ellen sighed, muttering, "So, is anyone having *fun* yet?"

"PUT me down for another shot because this is just *so* much fun," Jason muttered.

Kip knew he had to do something before that blasted woman ruined the evening with her damned competitive ways. If she wasn't so hard-headed and annoying, she'd actually be just his type. Legs that went on forever, the toned, fit body of an athlete, glorious dark-brown hair that cascaded to her waist in a silky waterfall, and eyes that sucker-punched him every time he stared into them. He'd never seen eyes so beautiful. More of a tomboy than not, she didn't wear makeup. Frankly, she didn't need it. With long eyelashes as dark as her hair, it would be a shame to cover them with anything. And the shape of her eyes was sexy as hell, with a rich whisky color that was stunning. All accented with sweeping dark eyebrows he wanted to stroke.

Every time he started to entertain the idea of seducing her, she opened her mouth and reminded him of what a bad idea that would be. Ellen was cute as hell, but he would be afraid of breaking her in two. Not to mention it would take way too much work to tame that Tasmanian devil. While gorgeous Samantha was taken by his best friend. No, natural-beauty Amber was definitely much more his speed than any woman he'd met in a very long time, but he couldn't read her, and had no idea if she was a one-night-stand sort of woman. After everything he'd been through, that was all he was looking for when it came to women.

For the first time since he'd planned this trip, he was beginning to regret placing them in such a secluded romantic setting. Calling them all to the tables in the middle of the room, he challenged them to some games. Amber, being the competitive sort that she was, didn't refuse for once, just like he'd known she wouldn't. Maybe *finally* they would have a good time.

For the next hour, Kip had them playing a game of poker. He and Amber went neck and neck, winning hand after hand, until Ellen got bored and tried to turn the game into one of strip poker. Jason finally perked up, but Nate put the kibosh on that. When they all quit, Ellen led them in a drinking game for the next hour. Once again, Amber tried to drink him under the table. Sam and Ellen had long since bowed out, with Amber beating Jason and eventually Nate, until just the two of them were left. She might be an Amazon, but she was no match for Kip. For her own well-being, he decided to be the bigger person and quit, because he knew she was too stubborn to do what was best for her.

"I win!" she said, slapping her hand on the bar and setting her glass down with a loud thunk. "Say it."

He let out a breath. "Say what?"

"Come on. Congratulate me, you big caveman." She snickered.

He just shook his head at her. "Congratulations, Amber. You're awesome," he said sarcastically.

"I know. I kept trying to tell you, but you wouldn't listen, you stubborn stubborn man, you." She hopped off her barstool and wobbled for a second.

He reached out and grabbed her, catching her around the waist to steady her. She was fine to stand on her own, but he didn't let go. Damn, she felt good. He stared down into her eyes and got lost again in their mesmerizing pools. He had a slight buzz, but that was all, since his massive size made it nearly impossible to get drunk. Probably a good thing right now, because the woman softening in his arms and smiling up at him sleepily was tipsy enough for the both of them. She would hate herself come morning, but for now he planned to enjoy every second of it.

"Let's play another game," she said, stepping out of his arms a bit, but still standing close.

"I'm out," Jason said, rising from his bar stool and heading for the stairs. "Night all."

"Party pooper," Ellen hollered after him.

"Count us out too," Nate chimed in. "My bride-to-be has had enough." He scooped Samantha in his arms.

"Oh my," she said with a breathless sigh. "Maybe I haven't had *quite* enough just yet, Santa."

"I was hoping you would say that, Mrs. Claus. Feeling naughty, are we? I have the perfect punishment." He kissed her on the nose and made a beeline for the stairs, taking them two at a time, with her giggling every step of the way.

"Well, that's a fine how-do-you-do. Guess I'll take myself to bed," Ellen muttered, and ambled off to the stairs. "Come on, Captain, you can be my date," she said, grabbing a bottle of Captain Morgan along the way. "Hell, let's make it a three-some with your buddy Jack." She grabbed a bottle of Jack Daniels with her other hand and muttered, "I'll bet *you* guys know how to have fun at least," as she headed up the stairs.

"Guess that leaves just you and me," Kip said to Amber, shoving his hands in his pockets so he wouldn't do something stupid like touch her again. "What game did you have in mind?"

"Truth or dare," she blurted, and then blinked as though she'd surprised herself. She licked her lips and then bit her bottom one as she stared at his.

He suspected she wouldn't be softening toward him like this if she were stone-cold sober, and would undoubtedly be pissed at herself later, but he wasn't fool enough to ignore her. She intrigued the hell out of him. One minute sparring with him, and the next devouring him with her eyes like she wanted to eat him up for dessert. She kept him on his toes, and he had to say it was a hell of a turn-on.

"Hmmm…" He rubbed his jaw, mulling her proposition over, then opted to go for the chicken-shit route as he replied, "Dare." He didn't do truth. Truth could be way too painful.

"Hmmm, is right. A man with secrets he doesn't want revealed. Coward. Okay, then." She rubbed her hands together, looked around the room, and then glanced out the window. Her eyes widened and a slow grin crept over her face, making her look young and playful and pretty instead of her usual guarded, competitive frown. He liked her this way even though he knew it wouldn't last. She surprised the hell out of him by challenging, "Strip down to your underwear and run out in the snow."

A bolt of lust ran through him. He clenched his hands into fists, fighting harder not to touch her. She had no idea just how close she was to pushing him over the edge. He'd been around enough women to recognize that she would welcome his attention, but then she'd hate him in the morning. So he gave her fair warning as he said, "I would but I'm not wearing any underwear."

"Oh," she squeaked, her eyes dipping down until she yanked them back up, her face sobering. She raised her chin a notch, as though unwilling to back down or let him get the upper hand. "Um, well, just take your shirt off then." She had shed her warm-up jacket during the drinking game, and wore only a tank top and warm-up pants now. She crossed her arms in front of her self-consciously, apparently not realizing the action only emphasized her breasts.

Far be it for him to point that out. Instead, he couldn't resist egging her on. He sat back to enjoy the show as he said in a soft deep voice, "You sure, because I'd be happy to oblige. I just thought it fair to warn you."

"No, no. That's okay. Just your shirt will be fine," she quickly said, obviously sobering up enough to realize what she'd started, but he knew her. She was way too competitive to back down now, God love her.

He didn't say a word, just slowly unzipped his warm-up jacket and slipped it off. Grabbing the hem of his T-shirt, he pulled it over his head and tossed it aside, standing bare-chested in nothing but his loose warm-up bottoms riding low on his hips.

"Well, what are you waiting for?" she snapped, looking anywhere but at his naked chest.

He bit back a chuckle and headed for the front door. Jogging outside, he stood for a moment, the brisk air actually feeling good. He needed a minute to cool off his burning insides, not to mention going commando did little to hide what she was doing to him. When he got his body under control, he returned to the lodge.

Coming to a stop before her, he said, "My turn."

She swallowed hard and shrugged. "Fine. I can play this game too. You didn't want to share with me, so I'm not about to reveal anything to you. Besides, you don't scare me. I say *dare*. And you can cover up now."

"I'm good like this," he responded defiantly, leaving his shirt off. Like hell he didn't scare her. She wanted him as much as he wanted her. Now that he knew that, it would be a damn sight harder not to seduce her. Every fiber of his being said that would be stupid. The problem was he'd never been that smart. He slowly leaned into her and practically purred, "I dare you to kiss me."

She gasped, her mouth falling open, and she actually took a step back. "What?"

"You heard me… coward." He tried to fight his grin, but it was damn hard.

"You're crazy," she said with a scowl.

"And you're standing under mistletoe." He shrugged. "It seemed only fitting."

She looked up and frowned, but didn't say a word when she finally looked at him. Then her jaw clenched like he knew it would, and she lunged at him. Reaching up and taking his face in her hands, she pulled his head down to hers and pressed her lips hard against his. A jolt of electricity zinged through him, but then she pulled away all too soon, panting as hard as he was. "Satisfied?"

They stared at each other, neither wanting to admit what they had both just felt. He couldn't take it anymore. "Not hardly," he finally growled, his smile long gone as he pulled her to him, swooping down and covering her mouth hungrily with his own.

She froze as though in shock for a moment, but then softened beneath his hands. Not willing to be outdone, she let out a whimper and stood on his feet, wrapping her arms around his neck to plaster her body to his, knocking him back a step. He groaned deep in his throat, countering as he slid his arms around her, running one over her long back and settling the other on her tight bottom. He squeezed gently, pressing her harder against his arousal, the feel of her body in his arms making his heart pound. He deepened the kiss by slipping his tongue between her lips to caress and stroke hers.

God, she felt amazing and fit him like she'd been made to be his. She tasted like whisky and honey and something that was purely Amber. And that scared the hell out of him. What if she wanted more than this? He knew he didn't have it in him to give her anything more than one night. He knew she wanted him, but how much more did she want? Would she be okay with one night, or did she want more? She was just so hard to read, he couldn't take the chance until she was completely sober and he knew for sure.

Pulling back, he cursed softly and stepped away as he tried to catch his breath. She stared at him in shock and confusion, like she'd felt the same electricity he had, and she didn't have a clue what to do about it either. Hell, he wasn't even sure they liked each other, and they sure as hell probably wouldn't come morning.

"Now, *that's* a proper kiss," he said, trying to lighten the moment, but knowing it came across as cocky. That tended to happen when he hid behind his wall.

"It was okay," she said with a shrug, "but I'm tired. I'd say it was a tie." She kept staring at his lips.

"Maybe we can finish this later. We both know you can't play a game without having a clear winner," he said carefully, looking for a clue as to how she really felt.

"Maybe," she responded, her face suddenly flushing a becoming rose as she gathered up her jacket while not quite meeting his eyes. "But I wouldn't hold your breath. I'm pretty good at winning. I only kissed you like that the first time because you couldn't handle it if I gave you a *real* kiss, Scrooge

McDunky." She tossed that long hair of hers over her shoulder again, which he now realized was a defense mechanism.

"You're on," he responded carefully, as he picked up his own clothing and followed her to the stairs. "But Amber?"

She paused halfway up the steps and turned around to finally look at him. "Yes?"

"Be prepared."

"For what?"

"Next time I won't hold back."

CHAPTER 3

"Never, *ever* let me drink like that again!" Amber said the next morning, as she nursed a cup of coffee, wincing over every sound the caveman made as he prepared breakfast.

Of course she'd overslept, and he'd beat her to the punch in rising early. He claimed it was because he had to take care of his horse. Apparently he owned an old-fashioned horse-drawn sleigh, with bells and all, and knew how to take care of it. The man had many talents. She should have guessed he would have something that charming at a place like this, but she had to admit she didn't picture him as a hands-on sort of guy. With all his money, he could afford to hire people to do that for him. That fact that he didn't was admirable, and that just irritated her more.

On top of all that, he was now organizing a fabulous buffet. True to his word, they didn't have to cook, but she'd still have liked a hand in putting it all together. But no, he couldn't even allow her that much. Had to show her up every chance he got. So here she sat by the fire with Ellen and Sam, while he and Nate and Jason worked. Most women would love that, but Amber wasn't most women and had never been good at letting anyone take care of her. Especially not a caveman who looked way too good after last night.

"It's not like he got you drunk on purpose." Ellen snorted, popping two pain pills after her night with the Captain and Jack. "That was all you and your competitive ways, babe. Anyone with eyes and half a brain could tell the Jolly Blond Giant has a hollow leg. I mean, seriously, what were you thinking?"

"Obviously she wasn't," Sam said, while holding an ice pack to her temple. Too much alcohol and not nearly enough sleep, undoubtedly from her groom-to-be keeping her up most of the night.

"I definitely wasn't thinking or I never would have kissed him," Amber muttered, shaking her head at her stupidity, then grabbing the top of her scalp when it felt like it was about to fall off.

"You what?" Ellen shrieked, and all three women groaned.

Kip shot them a curious glance. When Amber's face flushed pink, a slow, cocky, knowing grin spread over his way-too-good-looking face. She scowled, and his grin broadened. If she had the energy, she would smack him.

"I knew things would work out if you just gave him a chance," Sam said, with stars of love still clouding her vision.

That had to be it, because otherwise she'd realize how ridiculous she sounded. No way in hell would Amber ever get tangled up with a man like Kip. Been there, done that, didn't end well. And Kip was way more her type than that guy had ever been. Besides, she remembered enough about last night to know he was dangerous to her heart. Hot as hell, more than willing, but completely opposed to commitment.

Not that she wanted a commitment, she told herself for the millionth time. But if she were really honest with herself, she would admit she only said that because she was tired of men making her feel like she was good in bed but not good enough to marry. All because they were intimidated by her and couldn't handle her showing them up, which only made her work that much harder at doing exactly that.

"Must be nice," Ellen said with a dreamy sigh. "Meanwhile I get stuck with Jason Moore—Boring with a Capital B at Large."

"Don't go getting excited, Sam," Amber responded. "And trust me Ellen, that kiss was anything but nice. It was a dare, that's all. After you guys left, we played truth or dare, and then went to bed."

Both women raised their brows, staring at her.

"Alone," Amber added pointedly.

"For now." Ellen winked.

"Come and get it," Kip called out.

"See, Amber," Ellen said on a choking laugh, "he wants you to come and get it."

"You are so bad," Samantha said, swatting her, but smiling just as wide.

"You *both* are bad," Amber grumbled, adding with a mumble half under her breath, "and I have a feeling I'm in big trouble."

* * *

HOURS LATER, after decorating the tree and baking cookies, they spent the afternoon filled with outdoor activities. They'd even gone for a sleigh ride, singing Christmas carols until they drove Jason mad. The sky grew dark and stormy now. Amber's headache had finally dissipated, the cold air feeling wonderful. She had to admit this ski lodge—a.k.a. romantic oasis—was simply gorgeous. Intimate and quaint, it had just the right amount of activities to keep the guests entertained, mixed in with plenty of spots both indoors and out for a romantic moment to occur. Rustic décor filled with modern touches meant to tease and titillate.

Kip might have shown her up at breakfast, but Amber had schooled his butt at skiing. He was good, but she was better, especially at moguls and jumps. Everyone else had skied on the basic trails, with Jason only managing the bunny hill and one run, before retiring to the lounge to enjoy a drink in front of the fire while surfing his ever-present smart phone. Ellen twisted her ankle. Amber suspected she did it on purpose out of boredom or to make her jealous to prove a point. Either way, it worked.

Amber hated that it bothered her to watch Ellen enjoy every second of Kip wrapping her ankle and settling her on a comfy couch in front of the windows, so she could watch everyone with a toddy in hand and an ice pack on her ankle. To make matters worse, Kip returned only to school Amber on the snowmobiles. He was a beast. She had to admit she was impressed, which only irritated her further.

They ended with making snow angels and partaking in a snowball fight with Sam and Nate. When Kip and Amber turned it into their own personal war, firing shot after shot at each other, Nate and Sam gave up and went inside. Amber and Kip barely noticed.

"Did we scare everyone away?" he finally asked, from behind a huge snowman he'd made.

"Looks like it. Is that your way of saying you surrender?" she asked, while hiding behind a snow fort she'd built.

"Just because you're hot doesn't mean you're getting off that easily, babe," his deep voice echoed in the eerily darkening evening, sending chills through Amber's body. Chills that had nothing whatsoever to do with the dropping temperatures.

Pushing her traitorous body's response aside, she responded, "Nice try, McDunky. You're not distracting me that easily." She peeked over the top of her fort, and a snowball sailed by her head, just missing her hat by a mere centimeter. She hopped up and rapid-fired one back just as he popped his Jolly Blond Head up to see if he'd struck gold.

Smack!

He grunted and fell back with a moan.

"McDunky?"

Nothing.

"Caveman?"

Still nothing.

"Kip, quit messing around. Are you okay?"

When he remained silent, she started to grow concerned. The temperatures had dropped enough that the snow had started to turn icy. Heavy flakes fell down from the now black sky, making it hard to see beyond a foot in front of her face.

She cursed under her breath and jogged over to his side. Just as she cleared the snowman, he popped up and tackled her, pinning her down flat on her back beneath his massive body. He dusted her cheeks with snow, and she gasped from the cold.

"Gotcha. Cry uncle, and I'll let you up," he said, in that deep sexy voice of his.

"You rat! I thought you were hurt," she snapped, wiggling beneath him to no avail.

"You nailed me in the eye. Trust me I'm hurt. How am I going to explain my black eye next week?"

Her face hardened, and she stiffened beneath him. For a moment, she'd dared to have hope, but just like all the other men in her life, he'd ended up being intimidated by her. "God forbid you tell them a girl did it. Heaven forbid you let them know an actual woman beat you at something. Which is exactly why that kiss last night never should have happened. Get off me. I'm ready to go inside." She turned her head to the side.

He stilled for a moment. "Easy, Amber," he said softly, turning her face back to look at him. He was frowning down at her. "Someone really did a number on you, didn't they? I *meant* how will I explain the black eye to Nate's mother, let alone my own, at the wedding? It won't matter who did it. They won't be happy with me for ruining the wedding pictures." His face paled. "In fact, now that I think about it, Sam will probably kick my ass."

Amber relaxed beneath him, exhaling the breath she hadn't even realized she'd held. Hadn't realized just how much his explanation had meant to her, which was foolish because he'd made it clear he did *not* want anything serious. If anything happened between them, it would be purely physical. No emotions involved. She should walk away right now. Keep it light. Keep it simple. Keep her heart intact.

Instead, she responded, "You don't want to mess with Sam." Damn, but he unnerved her.

His gaze softened as it traced over her features. He pulled off his glove and wiped the snowflakes from her lashes and then did the most remarkable thing by tracing her eyebrow with his fingertip as though he'd been dying to do that. She felt it clear to the center of her soul.

"I find it sexy as hell that you challenge me in every way. Hell, you challenge me more than most men I know, and that's a huge turn-on for me. Make no mistake, that kiss did happen." He stared deep into her eyes. "And it's going to happen again."

He lowered his head with his eyes remaining open, holding her captive, giving her plenty of time to say no. She didn't move a muscle. He gently pressed his lips to hers. Sensations coursed through her until she blinked her eyelids closed and threw her arms around his neck, tilting her head and thrusting her tongue between his lips. He growled deep in his throat, sliding a leg over hers between her thighs, while touching and tasting every part of her mouth with his tongue. Pulse points long since forgotten came to life inside Amber's body, as her heartbeat quickened and she strained to arch her back and get closer to him. Recognizing her need as matching his own, he slid his large gloveless hand beneath her heavy jacket and sweater until he touched bare skin.

She gasped and he murmured words of encouragement as he rained kisses at the corners of her lips, across her cheeks and down her throat. His hand inched higher, and suddenly her chills were gone. Goosebumps were still there, but for an entirely different reason. She suddenly realized she'd never wanted anyone more. His long fingers had almost reached her breast when the world around her faded to black, literally, and the door to the lodge burst open.

"The power went out, and we're in a state of emergency!" Jason blurted. "A blizzard just hit the entire northeast coast.

Wait a minute, are you two okay? Why are you on the ground?"

Kip lifted his head, and Amber could barely make out his features. How had they completely shut out the world around them and not noticed the storm raging outside? Probably because the storm raging within them had been even bigger.

Kip cursed as he rolled off her and sat up, snapping her out of her haze of desire and back to reality. "We're fine," he snapped.

"What exactly does that mean?" Amber asked, clarifying, "The state of emergency, not the 'we're fine' part."

Kip pulled her up with him and took a breath that somehow sounded foreboding. "That we're snowed in," he answered gravely, looking a bit worried. "With no help and no way out."

"For how long?" she asked, taking a step back as she just now realized what that could mean.

"No way to tell, but we're not going to panic. We have plenty of supplies, and we are all capable adults. Plus there's a generator. It's no big deal, really," he sounded calm, but more like he was reassuring himself as much as her.

"It *is* a big deal, and we're so not fine, you rockhead." She punched him in the arm. "I knew I shouldn't have let you distract me. In fact, I never should have listened to you in the first place. Do you know what this means?"

He rubbed his bicep. "That I'll have to put up with your crazy ways longer?" he asked, clearly sounding frustrated with her.

"That's the least of your worries, McDunky. This means that Nate and Sam might miss their own wedding," she paused to let her words sink in, and watched his eyes widen as realization dawned, then she put the nail in his coffin by adding, "and it will be all your fault."

"WHAT THE HELL! I can't believe she is blaming me for this," Kip said to the group as he paced in his long johns, his hair hanging wild and free, probably making him look like a savage, but he didn't care. The damn woman made him feel like a savage. The rest of them sat in their thermal gear around the fire in the lodge an hour later, after getting the generator started.

Amber had started out this morning, hating that she'd kissed him—and liked it, no matter what she said—the night before. So she'd hoisted her defensive wall back up and ignored him in the morning until her competitive streak forced her to compete with him in the afternoon. She'd acted all tough, but he could tell she was in her element and having the time of her life. Then she'd finally let down her guard and warmed up to him as they'd shared such an amazing moment outside just a short while ago. Only now she'd turned back into an icicle the moment reality set in.

"Believe it, McDunky," she snapped, stepping in front of him like a defiant Amazon Goddess and poking him in the chest with a toss of her long hair. "You knew how much getting married on Christmas Eve meant to both Sam and Nate. Their special day shouldn't have to be on any other day. But now we're all stuck here in this godforsaken place because you had to go and be a cocky scrooge, only thinking of yourself and what *you* wanted."

"I'm losing money by closing down this place. I'd hardly

call that thinking of myself." He poked her right back, and she gasped, rubbing her shoulder through her ribbed top. "I did this for everyone, including you, Ms. I-have-to-outdo-everyone Stubborn. And I'd hardly call this place godforsaken," he growled back, then threw up his hands. "How the hell was I supposed to predict a blizzard would hit and snow us in?"

"It's called a weather map, genius. Maybe if you'd consulted one instead of having to control every blessed thing, we wouldn't be here right now," she raised her voice, thrusting her face into his personal 'zone'.

"You're just mad that you kissed me... *again*." He leaned down, his nose a mere inch from hers.

"I didn't kiss you." She hoisted her chin a notch. "*You* kissed *me*, like the Neanderthal that you are."

"And you sure as hell didn't fight me off, ice princess," he hissed, in a dangerous low voice. "In fact, if I recall, you kissed me back. More like devoured me. I was beginning to fear for my life."

She scowled at him disgustedly. "Last I checked you were on top."

"With no complaints from you." He smirked.

"If you two are done verbally fornicating, maybe we should make a plan," Ellen interrupted from her perch by the window, with her leg still propped on a pillow and a drink still in her hand.

"Verbally fornicating?" Jason raised a brow at her. "How old are you, five?"

She rolled her eyes. "At least I'm not ninety-five, which is how old you act, Moore of More Boring Than Any Man I've Ever Met."

"Children," Samantha said, "please stop fighting. I can't take any more." And then she burst into tears.

"You all should be ashamed of yourselves," Nate boomed, and then he took his fiancé in his arms.

"He's right," Kip said, and looked at the group, feeling terrible. "I apologize. For bringing you all here, and for letting my staff go, completely isolating us from the rest of the world. With the state of emergency and roads closed, we can't go anywhere until the storm passes. And we can't walk or take the sleds or the sleigh because it's too dangerous with the zero visibility out there. I never should have taken a chance so close to the wedding." His gaze cut to Amber's. "And I am sorry for making advances toward you when they are clearly not wanted. It won't happen again."

She blinked in surprise, and he could have sworn a look of confused disappointment flashed across her face before she covered it up.

Finally, he turned to Nate and Sam. "But mostly I am terribly sorry for ruining your wedding."

"The wedding is still a couple of days away," Ellen said, with her usual pre-holiday spunk. "There's still time for the roads to clear."

"And there's still time to turn this trip around and have fun, if you'd all just get along," Sam said, sniffling and dabbing at her eyes with Nate's monogrammed handkerchief.

"We wouldn't trade being with you guys for the world, even when you act like toddlers," Nate added softly. "Being all together is the most important thing to us. And if we can't get married on Christmas Eve, it won't be the end of the world."

"Kip's not the only one who's sorry," Amber said at last, addressing the group. "I've been so bitter and stubborn, and well," her gaze settled on him, "just plain stupid. I can admit your advances weren't unwanted, I was just afraid." She took a breath before continuing, "But there's no reason to be afraid of a good friend. A friend doesn't hurt you. In fact, having such a good friend can come with many possible benefits. The rest is just gravy."

Kip's smile came slow and sweet. "With *definite* benefits," he replied, not daring to comment on the gravy.

Her smile matched his. "Glad we settled that so we can finally relax. And for the record, I hate games too." She winked, and then that look of stubborn determination that he'd come to adore entered her beautiful eyes as she turned to Nate and said, "Make no mistake, McScroogy. You and Samantha Darling are most definitely getting married on Christmas Eve. It's what she's always wanted, and as her maid of honor, I won't rest until I make that happen."

CHAPTER 4

KIP'S FOREHEAD PUCKERED CURIOUSLY. Amber never ceased to amaze him, and kept life interesting, but even he didn't have a clue where she was headed with this one. "How can they get married on Christmas Eve if we're stuck here?"

Her gaze cut to Jason. "Hey, Moore. I know I had a lot to drink, but if I'm not mistaken, didn't you tell Ellen she was going to hell because of her elfish ways during our drinking game last night?"

Jason frowned. "Yes, and the irritating elf threatened to sue me if I started to preach at her."

"Exactly!" Ellen shot her a death glare, and Amber quickly amended, "Not that you're irritating, Ellen. I just meant the Jason part." Amber approached Jason and massaged his shoulders where he sat hunched over his smartphone. A broad grin spread across her lips. "And how exactly would you be able to do that, McPreachy?"

His eyes widened, and the first smile Kip had seen the entire weekend lit up Jason's face as he responded, "Because I'm an ordained minister in my church."

"Bingo!" Amber said, with a sparkle in her eyes. "Last time I checked, ordained ministers can perform weddings, can they not?"

"That they can," he responded, looking impressed.

Amber beamed, and Kip admitted she won big this time, and he couldn't be more proud of her. Those other guys were idiots to let her go just because she intimidated them. She was special. A rare gem among women, and any man would be lucky to call her his own.

"You mean...?" Samantha started to say but couldn't get the rest of the words out through her trembling lips.

"Yes, Samantha Darling, I still get to make you my wife on the day you changed my life forever," Nathan finished, and then kissed her soundly on the mouth.

Ellen cheered and clapped her hands.

Jason rolled his eyes and tossed back a shot.

While Kip stared at the most amazing woman he'd met in a long time, standing tall and proud and beautiful before him. His heart squeezed painfully, and he suddenly realized she made him want a hell of a lot more than friends-with-benefits from her. She made him want the gravy, and that scared the hell out of him. She had the capability of cutting him wide open and making him bleed far more deeply than his ex-wife ever had. He should walk away. No, he should run and never look back. Here he was afraid she might not want a one night stand, but now he was terrified she'd never want anything more. Hell, he wasn't even sure what he really wanted either. He just knew he wanted her, and couldn't imagine letting her go anytime soon. He didn't know for sure what he was going to do about it, but he knew damn well where he was going to start.

She held out her hand. "Truce?"

He folded her hand in his much larger one and shook, but didn't let go as he responded, "Come on, friend. We have a wedding to plan."

She licked her lips and said, "You read my mind. Just think of all the benefits of working *together* instead of against one another for a change."

He stared at her mouth and finally said, "Now you're the one reading *my* mind."

* * *

"So does everyone know what they are supposed to do?" Amber asked an hour later with clipboard in hand, skimming the notes from their brainstorming session.

Kip had stepped aside and offered to let her take the lead, which had surprised her. If she were honest, she'd admit he'd amazed her many times over the past few days. Samantha had been right when she'd said there was a lot more to him if she'd just give him a chance and get to know him. He didn't date because he'd been hurt too, not because he thought he was better than anyone. He just had his defense mechanisms, same as she did. But beneath it all, he was one amazing man, and his ex-wife had been a fool.

"I'll make a business plan—I mean wedding plan—and organize how everything will go," Nate said, bringing her focus back to the task at hand. "We'll have the wedding right here in the great room. I can picture it all. And I'll work on my vows." His tender gaze settled on Sam, and she smiled back lovingly.

"I will sing and play guitar," Kip said, shocking Amber. She had no idea he knew how to sing and play guitar. The man was full of surprises, and very sweet. "I always keep one in my suite here," he went on. "I'll work on a new song just for you both, and I'm sure I can figure out the melody for Here Comes the Bride."

"I already know how to officiate a wedding, so I will keep working on finding us a way home, just in case we can make it out in time," Jason said, already scanning his smart phone again.

"I will work on my vows as well," Sam said with another smile for her groom. "And I can make the flower arrangements from all the gorgeous flowers scattered throughout our suites and the lodge. We should have enough to decorate the hall and for the girls to carry."

"I can cook, I just never have anyone to cook for," Ellen said, ignoring Jason's snort, earning him a scowl from Nate. He was the only one who hadn't learned to play nice. "This will be fun," Ellen said cheerily, and this time Jason refrained from saying a word, even though he looked like it was killing him. "I'll arrange our rehearsal dinner and make some special dishes for the wedding reception," she added. "Your staff left enough food to last a month and feed an army, Kip."

"Only the best for my friends," he said, and looked right at Amber when he winked, astonishing her yet again by not flirting with Ellen.

For once in her life a man had eyes only for her, and it felt wonderful. Amber felt her face flush and body warm with pleasure. This truce was turning out to be the best thing she'd ever agreed to.

"I'll also dig out the best tablecloths and napkins I can find, and make some party favors and centerpieces for the tables," Ellen finished.

"This all sounds perfect. I mean this *is* the kind of thing we do for a living," Amber said. "And I can sew. I will use the satin bed sheets for our dresses. We'll go simple, with toga style dresses for Ellen and myself, and a simple strapless A-line for Sam that I can measure, cut, and sew by hand in no time. There were several sets of sheets in each room in just about every color imaginable, if Kip doesn't mind my cutting them up."

"I'm at your disposal. You see anything you want, don't hesitate to take it," he said.

She had to tear her eyes away from his and keep her focus, though he made it extremely difficult to focus on anything other than taking him straight up to his bedroom and pouncing onto his righteous body. She cleared her throat. "I'm sure I can make satin sashes for the men to wear with the suits they came here in as well." Her gaze shot to Kip with alarm.

"No worries, babe," he said, and her heart fluttered. "I keep a suit on hand here as well, just in case the need for one should arise. I'd say you pretty much have everything covered. Great job in planning this, by the way."

His smile and the tone of his voice rang true and sincere, which warmed her heart more than he could ever imagine. He really did respect her, and he didn't seem intimidated by her in the least. In fact, he seemed impressed. She knew he wanted her, and she definitely wanted him and all the benefits their friendship could withstand, but for the first time she wished they could play for keeps. Because it was going to hurt like hell to let him go after their time in Fantasyland came to an end.

"Okay, team. Let's get busy," Amber said, refusing to dwell on the certainty of the pain that was to come, focusing instead on the anticipation of the pleasure that was yet to happen. Locking gazes with Kip, no words were necessary to know he felt exactly the same way.

THE NEXT AFTERNOON Amber stood in the great room surveying the scene before her. She couldn't believe the progress everyone had made. They'd worked late into the night and wouldn't stop until they finished today. Tomorrow was Christmas Eve, and they had planned the wedding for the morning. She almost hoped they wouldn't get rescued, proud of all they had accomplished in such a short amount of time, simply by working together out of friendship and love. There had been no stress in planning the wedding this time, nothing but joy and laughter and memories they would never forget.

Nate had arranged all of the tables on the right and left of the room, leaving the center open as an aisle. There was no need for guest chairs, because the wedding of the year had turned into an intimate, private ceremony. At the end of the aisle, Jason had constructed an altar in front of the massive glass windows with the stunning view.

The raging storm gave off an eerie glow, and the snow fell in huge fat flakes, making it seem as though they were cocooned in a snow globe. The power was still out, but the generator continued to work. They'd covered all the tables, as well as the altar, with every candle they could find, so that it wouldn't matter if the generator quit during the ceremony.

Nate had found a plush throw rug in white and placed that

in front of the altar for them to stand on. Samantha had fashioned gorgeous flower bouquets of different colored roses for the girls to carry, as well as creating stunning flower arrangements of Vermont's most beautiful wildflowers, and had arranged them on the sides of the altar as well as all of the tables. Ellen had found white lace-covered satin tablecloths and napkins, heart-shaped chocolates, and bowls of strawberries that she placed as party favors on each table, as well as the best dishes and champagne glasses the resort had to offer.

Nate and Sam were busy working on their vows, now that the other details had been taken care of, and Ellen was working on the food for the rehearsal they would run through later that day. Jason was still checking weather reports and trying to think of a way out, but the state of emergency, with roads closed and no unnecessary travel, remained in effect. Meanwhile, Kip had rigged up the lodge's security camera to videotape the ceremony, and he set his personal camera on a tripod, to take pictures by remote control as well. He was off putting the finishing touches on the song he planned to sing. They had each prepared a short speech to recite in place of readings.

The last and hardest job fell on Amber. She'd gathered beautiful king-size peach satin sheets, with enough material for dresses and matching sashes, as well as ivory sheets from the honeymoon suite and the matching lace curtains for a veil. She'd measured Ellen and herself, making simple toga-style dresses that fell to the floor just above their feet. Out of sheer coincidence, Ellen had brought peach nail polish, which they planned to give each other pedicures in the morning while getting ready, and go barefoot, with matching flowers in their hair.

She'd left Samantha for last, creating a simple strapless ivory dress, but covering the bodice with the same lace she was using for the veil and leaving the hem much longer in the back so it would create a lovely train. She found some Velcro in the party-supply room of the lodge, which worked perfectly to fasten the dress in the back of the bodice.

The measuring, cutting, and fashioning of Ellen's and her own dress was simple. It was the hand-sewing of Sam's dress that took the most time. She whipped through the bridesmaid dresses first, and then focused on Sam's, just finishing this morning. Now she needed to measure each man and throw together three quick sashes in the same peach, since the color matched Nate's black, Jason's brown, and Kip's gray suits. She quickly measured the first two, saving the best for last.

And she knew exactly where to find him.

Quickly making her way down the hall, she stood just outside his bedroom door, suddenly nervous. Sparring with him was easy. She'd done it for the past year now. But this truce made her much more vulnerable. She had yet to step foot inside his master suite. Her suite had been amazing, so she could only imagine what his must look like as the owner of the lodge. Gathering her nerve, she knocked once. He hollered for her to come in over the noise of guitar notes, and she opened the door.

Breathtaking came to mind as she looked around the room. It was huge, with rich dark wood and the deep fall colors of Vermont leaves when they changed each fall. Not to mention a full-sized hot tub sat next to the window with the best view she'd seen yet. Very manly, and sexy as hell, without a single feminine touch. That reminded her he was a bachelor and intended to stay that way, but she had known that going into this. So she stepped through the door with no regrets and no false illusions that this was anything more than it was.

He sat in the center of his massive bed, wearing sweatpants, a dry fit T-shirt, and bare feet. His thick blond hair was pulled back in his standard ponytail, with a pencil behind his ear, his acoustic guitar on his lap, and an open notebook before him. When she remained silent, he finally looked up, his intense gray gaze heating when he saw it was her. He didn't say a word, just set his guitar down and stood, then slowly walked toward her.

Her heartbeat began to race as he approached her, looking like a predator, muscles bunching and flexing with every step. She licked her lips. "I, um, I need to measure you," she said, holding out her tape measure like a doofus. She was good at everything she did, but when it came to men and sex and seduction, she felt so inept. So not sexy.

He stopped before her, a breath away but not touching, as he looked down at her. His breathing quickened and his nostrils flared, his gaze holding her captive. He took the tape measure from her hand gently and tossed it aside, then closed the door behind her, locking it. Finally, he responded in a gruff voice, "And I need you."

"Oh, um, need me to what?" She felt like an idiot. It wasn't like it was her first time, but he made her feel different than any other man ever had. He made her feel special, like he wanted her more than he'd ever wanted anyone, which was crazy. He would have told her, but he hadn't. She couldn't let herself think that way. She couldn't let herself hope for more.

"I need you to make love to me while I worship you," his voice grew deeper, sexier, more gritty. But he still didn't touch her. Yet he looked at her like she truly was sexy and beautiful and the only woman on Earth that he wanted right now.

"I see." She swallowed hard. "And, um, when will that worshiping take place?"

"When you say you want me, too." He looked intense and scary and intimidating, like he wanted to eat her alive, yet she knew in her heart he wouldn't lay a hand on her unless she said he could. No, unless she said that she *wanted* him to. "I won't seduce you. You have to say that you want me as much as I want you. So tell me, princess. Why did you really come to my bedroom?"

She stared at him for an endless moment, swallowed hard, and then reached up to pull the pencil from behind his ear and toss it aside to join her tape measure, followed quickly by the small band holding his ponytail. His hair tumbled wild and free and savagely to his shoulders, making her pulse race with excitement.

She finally responded, "Because I want you to make love to me while I worship you, too." She felt more confident and more in control and more like herself. "If you don't touch me now, I'm going to ravish you, whether you like it or not."

A slight grin tugged at the corners of his full lips, and he growled, "Oh, I like it, love. Make no mistake about that." He bent down and swept her up in his arms as if she weighed nothing at all, and for the first time in her life she felt delicate and petite. She felt like his princess, and he was her knight in shining armor. She might not get her happily ever after, but she would damn sure get her happily right now.

CHAPTER 5

AMBER FELT time still as Kip carried her to his bed. His arms were so big and strong as they cradled her so tenderly against his massive chest with her arms looped around his thick neck. He set her on her feet to stand before him. Taking a step back, he just looked at her. Every inch of her, until she began to squirm with more need and desire than she'd ever felt.

"What do you want?" she asked, feeling a bit bashful. It was still broad daylight, and she'd never felt that she looked sexy. With a figure more like an athletic boy's than a woman's, she'd never really had curves. Not to mention her breasts were small, but at least they were perky.

"You know what I want," he said with a husky voice, staring down at her like a fierce warrior. Fierce and capable of taking whatever he wanted, yet so gentle and tender and full of restraint.

She'd known exactly what he wanted, she had just been stalling. "Maybe we could close the blinds?" she asked hopefully. He was godlike and she so was not. It was intimidating.

He didn't say a word, just shook his head no.

"Why?"

"I want to worship you, remember?" He cupped her cheek with his big palm. "You're a beautiful woman, Amber. Never doubt that." His captivating gray eyes spoke the truth and his deep voice rang with sincerity.

She covered his hand with her own and squeezed, in thanks for making her *feel* beautiful, then she lowered his hand slowly and reached for the edge of her shirt. Watching his eyes the entire time, she raised her T-shirt over her head and tossed it aside. Then she pushed down and stepped out of her warm-up pants, kicking them away. She stood for a moment in her sports bra and boy shorts. No cute, silky matched set like Samantha would wear, or barely-there sexy numbers like Ellen owned, if she chose to wear any in the first place. Amber preferred a supportive yet comfortable set that wouldn't hinder her in a competition, should one arise.

"Sorry," she muttered. "It's all I own."

The corner of his mouth hitched up slightly. "It's perfect." His eyes met hers. "You're perfect. Now it's my turn."

He whipped off his T-shirt, the muscles in his arms bulging with every movement. Then he pushed down his pants, and she gasped. "What can I say, other than my birthday suit is all I own."

"You have a very nice birthday suit," she barely got out as she tore off her bra and reached for her panties.

He stilled her hands with his own. "Let me," he said, the teasing note in his voice gone.

Her gaze settled on his, but his eyes were locked onto her breasts, worshiping her with a mere look. If she'd had any doubts about how much he truly wanted her, they were long gone now. Her chest rose and fell, her nipples hardening just from his hot gaze caressing them. Lifting his hands, he gently threaded them through her hair and sighed like he'd wanted to do that for a long time. He tipped her head back and kissed her neck as he ran his fingers down the long length of the strands, feeling its softness. That alone had him breathing heavier, which was a turn-on itself.

His tongue touched her ear, and he whispered soft words of endearment as he trailed his hands over her shoulders next. He let his palms run down the length of her arms until his fingers threaded with her hands for a moment, before settling on her waist. He pulled his head back to look at her as he slowly slid them up her ribcage and cupped her breasts.

She sucked in a breath, and he groaned, feathering his thumbs over her nipples before dropping down and taking one in his mouth to suck hard. Amber shoved her hands in his thick hair and cried out in pleasure, nearly coming undone. So many sensations were coursing through her body, building and amplifying with his every touch, every taste—she didn't think she could take much more, and they'd barely gotten started. It had never been this intense for her before. Never felt this right. Never felt so unbelievably special.

"Kip, I…"

"I know, baby, me too. Stay with me." He kissed his way down her belly and dropped to his knees before her.

Holding onto his shoulders because her knees were so weak, she didn't think she could support herself. She swooned when he circled her belly button with his tongue. His large hands nearly spanned her entire waist. He slid them lower, running them over her hips and grabbing her panties. He slowly peeled them down, kissing every inch of skin that was revealed along the way.

"Step out of these, sweetheart," he said, and when she did, her legs separated and he dove his tongue deep.

She screamed his name and convulsed, unable to stop the powerful waves of pleasure from consuming her. He never stopped caressing her with his tongue and lips and fingers, riding the wave along with her, and holding her to him when her knees gave out. When she was left quaking and weak, he rose to his feet, lifting her with him and carrying her to his bed. Her mind was numb and her body so full of satisfying tingles, it took her a minute to realize what had just happened, as he placed her in the center of the mattress and then lay down beside her.

"I'm so sorry," she said. He'd given her such intense pleasure, selflessly making sure she was fully satisfied, never once thinking about his own needs. He was so different from the man she had once thought him to be. She'd never before been touched and caressed and kissed so tenderly, with such passion and devotion. It made her want to cry with so many emotions stirring within her.

"Don't be sorry," he replied softly, tracing her face lovingly and bringing her gaze back to his. His eyes were heavy-lidded and full of lust and appreciation. "You let me worship you, and I've never seen anything more beautiful than you coming apart in my arms. You're lovely, Amber. Thank you for that."

"Oh, well, in that case you're welcome." She smiled slowly, fighting off the silly lump in her throat, and wanting desperately to return the favor. "Now it's only fair you keep your end of the deal."

"And that is..." He looked at her with anticipation and hope.

"You let me make love to you." She caressed his face and trailed a thumb over his full bottom lip.

He bit her thumb lightly, then licked and kissed it before responding, "With pleasure."

A thrill of empowerment ran through her as she rolled him over onto his back. She loved that he didn't need to prove his manliness around her. He wasn't intimidated by her in the least, and he was comfortable enough in his own skin to let her take the lead. That was sexier than anything else he could have done or said.

She got to her knees, straddling him, but didn't take him inside her just yet. She wanted to see his face, his expression, and know she could make him feel how he had made her feel. Reaching out, she ran her hands over his sculpted chest and rippled abs, marveling over the work of art the good Lord had created when he made Kip Covington.

"You're beautiful, you know," she said softly, and then she took him in her hand and stroked the long length of him over and over, teasing and touching him like he had her.

He pulsed and a deep growl left his throat. "Easy, love. It's been a long time."

"That only makes this all the sweeter," she replied, loving that he was more like her than she ever imagined. He wasn't a cocky playboy at all. He was a man who'd been hurt, same as her, and who deserved to be loved by someone who truly cared about him. She was just afraid she cared too much and would never be the same when this was over.

She couldn't think about that or she would fall apart. Couldn't let her doubts and fears ruin a memory she would cherish forever. She dropped down and took him in her mouth, loving him as tenderly and intimately as she could, trying to show him what she could never say in words. Just how much he had come to mean to her.

He threw back his head and shouted her name, pulling her up the length of him. "I need you, baby. So damn much. I want to be inside you now."

She crushed her mouth to his and kissed him deeply as she lowered herself onto the long length of him until she felt they were truly one. Lifting her head, she looked into his eyes as she began to move. A look of intense passion and wonder and something else she couldn't quite identify seared her to the core. He rolled them over, kissing her thoroughly as he picked up the pace and brought them both home. They cried out simultaneously as wave after wave consumed them, drowning them both in the purest pleasure imaginable.

In that moment, Amber knew without a doubt that a part of her was ruined forever. She'd gone and done the dumbest thing possible. She'd fallen in love with a caveman. The problem was she didn't think he'd ever be able to love her back, and she couldn't do a damn thing about it. That had been their deal, and she'd known that going in. No man had ever wanted her for his own, not for keeps anyway, and she hadn't expected this time to be any different. But she wouldn't make him feel guilty. She would just love him and enjoy him for the time they had left. But one thing was certain…

From this moment on, her life would never be the same.

* * *

LATER THAT EVENING, Kip went through the motions of the wedding rehearsal, followed by the impressive feast that Ellen had created for their dinner. Everything had gone perfectly, though he could hardly remember any of it. He couldn't stop thinking about making love to Amber. He'd had a few women throughout his life, and his sex life with his wife had been good, but no woman had ever made him feel the way Amber did. Making love to her had been a life-changing experience for him. There was no other way to describe it.

And he was in deep shit now.

He didn't know how he could let her go. She'd ruined him for anyone else. The way she gave so freely of herself, without holding anything back. She cared as much about pleasing him as she had about receiving her own pleasure. He truly cherished everything about her, and if he were honest, he always had.

Right from the start she had challenged him the way no other woman had. She'd kept him on his toes all year long. He'd called her and interfered with every move she made, basically being a pain in her ass, because something about her had drawn him in right from the beginning. Once he'd finally met her in person, he'd recognized why. He had a kindred spirit in her. He'd fought it. Tried like hell to deny it. But in the end, he'd succumbed to it and done the stupidest thing he ever could.

He'd fallen in love with a stubborn, defiant, Amazon Goddess.

So he was back to not knowing how to let her go, yet knowing he couldn't force her to stay. The beast within him wanted to throw her over his shoulder and lock her in his room for eternity, but the man his mother had raised would put her feelings first. She'd made it clear right from the start that she didn't want a long-term relationship any more than he did. They'd set rules, and gone into this knowing exactly what it was and what it wasn't. It wasn't fair for him to change the rules now. So he would love her the best he could while he still could, and then he would set her free. It would kill him, but he had no other choice.

He couldn't be with another woman who didn't really want to be with him.

"What's wrong?" Amber asked, coming to a stop beside him and crossing her arms in front of her.

He didn't ever want her to be insecure or hurt because of him. "Not a thing in the world," he said reassuringly with a wink.

"That's good. You looked angry and a little sad. I got worried you might regret earlier." Her whisky-colored eyes stared up at him with concern and doubt and a little sadness of their own, if he wasn't mistaken.

"That's not possible," he said, taking in every lovely feature on her perfect face.

"We make a pretty good team, I'd say." She relaxed. "I can't believe we pulled off in two days what we barely pulled off in an entire year."

"We make a great team. We just didn't know it before."

She looked at him curiously over the tone in his voice that he hadn't meant to expose. "And now that we do, what are you saying?" She bit her lip, and he couldn't tell if she was afraid he would or wouldn't say what was on his mind.

"What do you want me to say?" he asked, wondering if she was entertaining the same crazy thoughts he was, or if it was just wishful thinking on his part.

She looked like a deer caught in the headlights. "I..."

"Look up, you two," Ellen chirped, coming to a stop beside them. "You can't pass up mistletoe and not kiss. It's bad luck."

Amber blinked and then complied, looking surprised. "Mistletoe?"

"Lucky ducks," Ellen sighed. "I was hoping to meet a hot guy at the reception, but now that we're stuck here it looks like I'm stuck with Mr. Moore Boring. Screw that. I'm letting Captain Jack take me away from my misery. Toodles."

"Sorry. Ellen's a character," Amber said, regaining his attention. "You were saying?"

"Just that I intend to make the most of our time together, and Ellen's right. We wouldn't want to risk any more bad luck the night before the wedding."

"Ah, that's right," Amber responded, and a flash of something he couldn't quite identify crossed her face as she finished with, "our time here is almost up." Then she smiled a sexy smile and looked up at him through her lush lashes. "So what are you waiting for, caveman?"

"You should know by now, princess."

"Yes, McDunky, I want you to kiss me. Now, please."

"As you wish, milady. Who am I to deny an Amazon Goddess?" He took her in his arms, where he intended to keep her the rest of the night, and lowered his head to hers, pretending for a moment at least that she truly was his to keep.

CHAPTER 6

THE NEXT MORNING was Christmas Eve. The day of the wedding, and everything was perfect. Well, almost everything, Amber thought with a lump in her throat. Last night had been breathtakingly beautiful, incredible... magical. She didn't want her time with Kip to be over, but she knew the storm would end soon, and reality return.

Fantasy officially over.

"You're amazing, Amber," Samantha said, staring at herself in the mirror. "The dress, the veil, my hair... all of it is perfect. And Ellen, what you did with the food and tables and favors is downright inspiring. I wouldn't trade any of this for the most elaborate wedding in the world." She turned to look at both Ellen and Amber. "You guys mean everything to me. Even if the roads clear, *this* is the wedding I want. Thank you both for making my dreams come true."

"You know we would do anything for you," Amber said.

"Yeah, you deserve the best," Ellen added. "And hey, the flowers rock."

"We do make a pretty good team." Sam smiled a little sadly.

"Promise me things won't change between us after I'm married?"

"That's music to my ears," Amber said, feeling relieved. "I was worried about exactly that. Trust me, we're not going anywhere."

"You just let McScroogy know we have visitation rights," Ellen chimed in, and pulled both Sam and Amber in for a bear hug.

"Don't make me smudge my makeup," Sam said, sniffling and dabbing at the corners of her eyes as she pulled away.

"At least you two have someone special in your lives," Ellen said. "I've got nothin' but you guys," she whined.

"I don't have anyone special in my life," Amber lied.

"We have eyes, honey," Sam added gently. "Everyone can see you and Kip were made for each other."

"Doesn't matter." Amber turned away to inspect her dress and hide her feelings. These were her best friends, and they usually shared everything, but her feelings were too raw right now. "Neither one of us wants a relationship, so it is what it is. When this is over, I'll have nothing but you two as well, and that's fine by me."

"If you say so," Ellen said.

"Have you told him how you really feel?" Sam asked softly.

"I hear the music. That's our cue," Amber said, and led the way out the door and down to the great hall without daring to look back.

Since Nate was the groom, and Jason was officiating, and Kip was playing guitar, Amber and Ellen were both going to give Sam away together. The Three Musketeers' final stand.

"This is it," Ellen said.

"Ready?" Amber asked.

"Absolutely," Sam answered.

The women flanked her sides, and the three of them walked down the aisle to the sound of Kip strumming the soft chords of Here Comes the Bride. Amber got a lump in her throat at the look on Nathan's face, as his eyes filled with love and awe when he gazed upon Samantha. For once, Jason wasn't looking at his smart phone, but he *was* studying his notes for officiating. Then Amber's gaze settled on Kip. He looked so handsome.

She sucked in a breath. He stared at her so intensely, watching every step she took with a look of something she was afraid to identify. Because if she was wrong, it would be worse than him never loving her at all. So she did what she always did—guarded her heart and looked away, refusing to hope for anything more than affection and respect from him.

Coming to a stop before the altar, Amber and Ellen kissed Sam's cheeks and handed her off to Nate. Nate took Sam's hand, and they stepped up to the altar before Jason. Over the next half hour, each of them took a turn giving their speeches in place of readings, bringing tears of joy to Sam and causing Nate's eyes to mist with happiness. And when Kip sang the song he wrote for just the two of them, Ellen broke out with sniffles.

Through it all, Amber remained strong, rejoicing in her friend's happiness, but refusing to give in to grieving for the loss of her own. The vows Sam and Nate wrote for each other nearly did her in, but still she didn't break down. She was afraid if she started, she'd never be able to stop. And that wouldn't do anyone any good. She did this to herself, and she wasn't about to make Kip uncomfortable. He hadn't done anything wrong. He'd given her some amazing memories. It wasn't his fault she'd fallen in love with him when she'd led him to believe she wouldn't.

Jason finished, and finally pronounced Nathan and Samantha man and wife. And then the most miraculous thing happened. The remnants of the storm finally stopped, and the sun came out, as though blessing their union. It was the most beautiful thing Amber had ever seen. Like the entire universe knew what they had was special. She couldn't help but be human, and long for something more. Blinking furiously, she struggled to keep the tears at bay.

"Are you okay?" Kip asked, drawing her eyes to him at last. She hadn't realized he'd moved beside her.

"Yes—no—I don't know," she managed to get out past the lump in her throat. How had everything become such a mess?

"Amber, there's something I—"

The power surged back on, and Jason shouted, "Yes!" while staring at his smart phone. "The storm's over and the state of emergency has been lifted. It looks like a lot of the roads have already been cleared. Your lodge was just located in the last area where the storm had lingered. It's like we were cut off in our own little snow bubble while the rest of the world went about their lives, business as usual. A ton of people have been trying to get in touch with us about the wedding plans."

"What does that mean?" Amber asked, feeling as though they'd come full circle.

"That we can still make Nate and Sam's reception, thank God!" Ellen said. "Don't get me wrong. You're all great, but I really want to find a man of my own. No offense, Jason."

Everyone laughed, except for Jason of course.

"Kip, call everyone and tell them the party's still on," Nate said. "We paid for it—we might as well use it. Besides, I'd like to show off my new wife." He kissed Samantha lovingly on the lips.

"Your wife." Samantha beamed with happiness. "I love the sound of that, husband." But then she frowned. "Except how are we going to get out of here?"

"I can take us out of here on the sleigh and have the limos meet us at the main road by my neighbor's farm, if everyone's game," Kip said, and looked straight at Amber. "Unless anyone objects to moving on?"

She smiled stiffly and replied, "Not at all. Moving on sounds great to me. Let the sleigh bells ring."

THE RECEPTION WAS HELD at a gorgeous country club that Nathan belonged to in Boston. They didn't bother to pack, figuring they would send for their things later. They all climbed into the sleigh, and it had taken a half hour to reach Kip's neighbor's farm where he left his horse in good care. Three and a half hours later, the limos reached the club. It was late afternoon, and the guests were all there, ready and waiting to toast the bride and groom.

Just as Kip had imagined, Sam's mother, along with Nate's, hadn't been thrilled with his lingering black eye from Amber having nailed him with an icy snowball. But Sam had covered most of it with makeup. She was so happy to be married; nothing bothered her. Kip had brought the wedding video and his camera with him, which went a long way in smoothing things over with the mothers as they watched in tears. And Nate and Sam promised that on their first anniversary, they would renew their vows in front of everyone.

Meanwhile, the guests were seated and dinner had been served. Prime rib, fancy chicken dishes, lobster... you name it, Nathan had supplied it. Only the best for his bride. He'd even had the place decorated in a Christmas theme, of course, adding a sleigh bell to every table as a party favor. Kip sipped fine champagne and smiled over how happy Nate and Sam looked, then he glanced beside Sam and frowned when his gaze landed on Amber. She was civil and pleasant enough toward him, but a wall had definitely been raised between them. It pissed him off. Last night she had been the most amazing and loving woman in his arms. What they'd shared between them had been mind-blowing, incredible... *special*.

For her to act so casual now killed him.

He'd never had a woman respond so amazingly to his every touch, every kiss, every murmur. Her body didn't lie, and what he had seen in her eyes had to have been real. It had said what she couldn't, and had given him hope. Or so he'd thought. For a stupid moment, he had actually thought maybe, just maybe, there could be more between them. But then she'd turned back into the ice princess with the light of day.

Dammit, he'd promised himself he'd be gracious and gentlemanly and let her go when the time came. She obviously didn't want anything more from him than friendship, the benefits clearly over, now that they had left the lodge. He'd even tried to broach the subject with her, just to see if maybe she could come to feel something more for him, but she kept changing the subject and cutting him off. Like she didn't want to hear he had feelings for her. Hell, what he felt for her went a damn sight deeper than mere feelings.

He was in love with her.

But given the way she was acting, telling her how he felt

would probably push her over the edge. He'd known the rules going into this, he just hadn't anticipated how hard this would actually be. And damned if he didn't care more about not wanting to upset her, than the heartache it would surely bring by keeping silent and letting her go. But let her go he would, because it was the right thing to do. He swallowed hard over the lump in his throat and the ache in his chest.

The sound of a ringing sleigh bell snapped him out of his dark depressing thoughts. He blinked to see Amber stand up and raise her glass. He couldn't help smiling a little sadly as his competitive Amazon Goddess beat him to the punch one last time in giving her toast to the bride and groom. Cursing softly, he realized he was going to miss this. Miss her.

"Hello, everyone." Everyone said hi, and she cleared her throat as though struggling with emotion. "I just want to take this moment to thank you all for coming. Nathan and Samantha's love is a miracle. A year ago she saved him from himself, and in return he gave her his heart. Their whole wedding was a miracle. I didn't think Kip and I would ever manage to see eye-to-eye on planning the first wedding. But something changed at the lodge."

Her voice broke, and his heart twisted painfully. If only she would look at him, yet she still didn't. She just composed herself and kept talking, "Somewhere along the way, we became friends. Very special friends." Her voice softened. "And once we all worked together, we managed to pull off a miracle of our own. We gave Sam and Nate the wedding of their dreams, and it was amazing. *They* are amazing together. I know I will never forget these past few magical days."

Her voice wobbled and she never once made eye contact with Kip. "I know Nate and Sam will make each other blissfully happy for the rest of their lives because they are a perfect match. A love like theirs is special. It's unique and rare and only comes along once in a lifetime. Sadly most of us will never achieve what they have, so raise your glasses and help me say cheers to Sam and Nate."

"No," Kip said, surging to his feet and surprising himself. "That's bullshit," he couldn't seem to stop the words from bursting out of his chest on a growl or erase his scowl.

Gasps echoed throughout the room.

He forcibly tried to relax his features and calm himself. "Yes, Nathan and Samantha have a magical and special kind of love, and I wish them the best. Truly, I do." He raised his glass to them in salute, and then narrowed his eyes as he looked at Amber, the stubborn yet wonderful woman who held his heart and his happiness in the palm of her hand. "But dammit, it's not true that we'll never achieve what they have. If you'd stop being so stubborn and open your beautiful eyes, you would see we already have it."

She still wouldn't look at him, but he saw her start to blink rapidly, and then the first big tear rolled down her cheek. Finally, blessedly, her wall began to crumble and real raw emotion seeped out.

"Amber, look at me, baby," he said softly. When she finally complied, his own voice broke as he said, "I love you so damn much." Her lips parted, but she couldn't speak. She just started crying harder, earning him scowls from both Samantha and Ellen. He vaulted over the head table to stand before her with the table between them. "I know I'm breaking the rules, and I know you think I'm a caveman, and I know I don't deserve you, and you'll probably never come to love me, but I—"

"You talk too much," she finally said with a sniffle and a slight smile, her cheeks soaking wet but shining bright.

"I do?" he asked hopefully.

"No," she said softly, and added in the most tender, loving tone he'd ever heard from her, "I do."

"You do what?" he asked suspiciously. "Talk too much?"

"Love you too, you caveman." She laughed. "And there'd better be a proposal in there somewhere, because I've waited too long for a man like you."

His lips parted and his heart filled with love for this gorgeous creature standing proud and tall and vulnerable before him. He would spend the rest of his life showing her he wanted her for everything. For more than he'd ever wanted anyone in his entire life. He wanted her to be his and only his forever. But she had to want him too, not just what he stood for. "You seriously want to marry me? I mean, I was hoping you would eventually come to love me, but you actually want to be my wife?"

"More than you'll ever know. I was just terrified to break the rules and tell you. And babe, I don't care about who you were, because I know exactly who you are. You're mine."

"I have been for a year. You just didn't know it." He stared deep into her eyes as he said, "I can't believe we both almost sacrificed our own happiness in trying to set each other free. Amber Evans, will you do me the honor of becoming my wife, and love me and challenge me and keep me on my toes for the rest of my days?"

"Yes!" she shouted, and then threw herself at him, kissing him soundly on the mouth to the cheers of the room. He lifted her into his arms, not wanting to let her go. When she finally pulled away, she whispered for his ears only, "For the record, I asked you first."

He burst out laughing, then said softly, "God, I love the hell out of you. And for the record, I said it first."

"You win." She sighed dreamily, looking at him like he was the only man for her, and he knew in his heart she would never love another. "Just promise me you won't stop saying it ever?" she added.

"Deal. And I'd say we both just won." He pressed his lips against hers, taking her back into his arms, where he never intended to let her go.

ABOUT THE AUTHOR

Kari Lee Townsend is a National Bestselling Author of mysteries & a tween superhero series. She also writes romance and women's fiction as Kari Lee Harmon. With a background in English education, she's now a full-time writer, wife to her own superhero, mom of 3 sons, 1 darling diva, 1 daughter-in-law & 2 lovable fur babies. These days you'll find her walking her dogs or hard at work on her next story, living a blessed life.

ALSO BY THE AUTHOR

COMFORT CLUB SERIES

Sleeping in the Middle

MERRY SCROOGE-MAS SERIES

Naughty or Nice

Sleigh Bells Ring

Jingle All The Way

LAKE HOUSE TREASURES SERIES

The Beginning

Amber

Meghan

Brook

www.ingramcontent.com/pod-product-compliance
Lightning Source LLC
Chambersburg PA
CBHW020142120726
47903CB00007B/2379